EVERTASTER

The Buttersmiths' Gold

Adam Glendon Sidwell

EVERTASTER

The Buttersmiths' Gold

FUTURE HOUSE PUBLISHING

Copyright © 2013 Adam Glendon Sidwell

Cover art: Seth Hippen

Title design: Matthew Eng

Inside Illustrations: Adam Glendon Sidwell

All rights reserved.

ISBN: 0989125300
ISBN-13: 978-0-9891253-0-7

The Buttersmiths' Gold

FOREWORD

This book is about Torbjorn and Storfjell. If you know who they are, read on. If you don't, this is as good a time as any to find out, and an excellent place for you to enter the Evertaster world. Guster and the Johnsonvilles, the main characters in the Evertaster series, however, aren't in this story, since this story happened long before they were ever born.

Not to worry though! I'll tell you what happens to Guster in *The Delicious City* and *the Final Season*. Those books continue the main storyline in the Evertaster series and follow the Johnsonvilles through to their bitter or blessed end. I'm working on those books even as I write this foreword. I hope you're hungry for them.

The Buttersmiths' Gold, on the other hand, is a companion novella – it provides insight into the One Recipe, hinting at its destiny and telling secrets that aren't told anywhere else but in these pages. It is a must-read for those who want to know the One Recipe's history. *The Buttersmiths' Gold* – the book you hold in your hands – is a story that just had to be told, about two characters that absolutely would not remain silent about their adventurous past and how it changed their people forever.

It takes many hands to finish a book, and this one wouldn't be here without all those fingers.

A big thanks to Alyssa Henkin, my agent at Trident Media Group, who always provides indispensable editorial insight.

Thank you to Jarom Sidwell, who put incredible efforts into telling the world about the Evertaster series before anyone knew what it was.

Thanks to my beta-readers: Gentle Ben, Kimberly Chambers, Jarom, JP Boyd, Michelle Sidwell, Q and Cheatham the Destructor. Thanks to Noelle Tomlinson, a very old friend from the days when we first learned to read real books. She's a dedicated librarian.

And thanks to Seth Hippen, the most awesome artist in our animation class way back when at BYU. He painted the cover art. Quick! Turn to the front cover right now so you can look at it one more time. Marvelous!

Thanks to Matthew Eng, an excellent artist and friend who did the magical title design.

And thanks to Catherine Barnhill, who is a very smart copy editor and a good friend. She's saved the day on more than one occasion.

Finally, thanks to you, the gentle reader who dared pick up this book to find out what story it holds inside.

Enjoy the taste!

Adam Glendon Sidwell
Los Angeles, California, March 2013

This book is dedicated to FJ, who loves Nectar of Moo more than any little snuggler I've ever met.

Chapter 1 — Torbjorn and Storfjell

Almost every historian you ever meet will tell you that there is nothing Vikings love more than blueberry muffins. Blueberry muffins with blueberries shining like gems atop the muffin's golden crown. Blueberry muffins with little bubbles of succulent blue juice that burst in your mouth when you sever their skin with your teeth. Blueberry muffins for breakfast, blueberry muffins for lunch, blueberry muffins for supper next to your clan's roaring fire in the longhouse.

Most historians would tell you that's what Vikings love most. Most historians would be wrong.

"You boys sure seem to love muffins more than anything!" said Braxton. The old pilot had seen it all in his day – kangaroo rodeos, bees on bicycles, and even a fish who could shoot – but never ever in his whole life did he expect to be stranded on board a wooden ship in the middle of the sea with a pair of humongous Vikings.

And now that pair had laid aside their horned helmets and were shoveling blueberry muffins into their mouths by the fistful.

"Oh yah! ha ha!" laughed the larger of the two Vikings – his name was Storfjell – with a deep, rumbly laugh that shook his mountainous belly. Golden-brown muffin crumbs fell from Storfjell's mouth into his silvery beard. He was at least eleven feet tall, with a pair of silver braids that must have been woven from moonbeams. "What you are saying is a common mistake! We are loving blueberry muffins very much! But you know what we are loving even more?" Storfjell said between mouthfuls.

Braxton's watery eyes twinkled. The cows mooed. "I could venture a guess," he said. If it weren't for these two Vikings, alive and thriving in the modern era, unknown to the rest of the world, Braxton might still be stuck on a remote island in the Norwegian Sea. Still, as strange as it all was, he had a feeling he knew what they were going to say.

"Blueberry muffins are delicious to eat of course, but it is this, the Golden Fortune of our Herds – that is the best thing to taste in all of Midgard!" said the Viking named Torbjorn. Torbjorn was the smaller of the two – he was still ten feet tall and broad as an ox. He heaved a heavy wooden barrel upright and slid it across the deck of the ship to the mast where they sat. He pried off the lid with his battle axe and dipped the edge of the blade into the soft, golden butter inside. "It is butter that we Vikings love all the best!"

Butter – creamy, rich and smooth. *I wonder what the encyclopedias would say about that,* thought Braxton. The way these boys drank down their butter, you'd think their butter was the treasure that launched the Viking Age itself. He watched their herd of cows pushing at the oars. A question began to form in Braxton's mind. There was something he had to know. "I know you love your cows and treat them right. I know you feed them on fresh clover," said Braxton. "But what is it that makes your butter so special?"

Storfjell smiled, his long silver mustache turning upward with the corners of his mouth. He looked quite pleased that Braxton would ask. "This is a good thing you have wondered, but it is not my story to tell." He pointed to his brother Torbjorn. "You must ask him, and he will tell you that and many things."

Torbjorn scooped out another mound of butter and smeared it all over the heap of muffins still left on the table, then pounded the lid back onto the barrel with the butt of his axe. He was usually the jollier of the two Buttersmiths, but now, all of a sudden, he grew quiet. "It is an ancient tale," he said. "One that begins with our fathers and their fathers' fathers, so many times ago, before the ships could cross the great sea, when there were fewer people on the land, and when kings were rare indeed."

Braxton took another bite of his muffin. The butter washed down his throat. He settled back against a barrel. It was a long way to land, and this was the tale he'd hoped would get told.

"In those days, our clan churned the butter in wooden churns by hand. It was a very tiring work.

"In those days, our clansmen did not live past 40 winters old. If he did not get a knife in his back, or a battle axe to his teeth, old age would surely find him.

"My father's father's father, very many fathers ago, was also like me named Torbjorn. Also his brother, like mine, was called Storfjell," said Torbjorn. His words went up and down in his sing-songy voice as he spoke. With the fresh muffin warming Braxton's belly from the inside, and the creamy butter melting through him and coating all his nooks and crannies, Braxton began to hear Torbjorn's words as if they were a dream. This is the story that Torbjorn told.

Chapter 2 — Smordal

Many centuries ago, young Torbjorn Trofastsonn of Smordal knew quite well that the tastiest thing in the whole world was butter. Creamy, rich and smooth. Butter was the reason his clan invented blueberry muffins in the first place – they'd needed something to smear it on. Butter was their lifeblood. Butter was the warmth in their hearts, the horns on their helmets, the tips of their mustaches.

Butter was also their greatest secret.

Torbjorn hoisted an oversized basket full of steaming hot muffins into his arms and tottered down the gangplank onto the sandy shore of Viksfjord, the merchants' village. He and his clan had sailed from the open sea into the fjord this morning, where he and his brother Storfjell had helped Father and the bovines row the final twenty miles to the sand.

He did not mind the work. He was large for only 13 winters old. Smaller than the biggest boulders, but larger than most respectable rocks, Torbjorn was already 8 feet tall. If five sheep stacked themselves on top of each other, he could stare the fourth one straight in the eye. He was from Smordal, and Smordaler were known for their tremendous size – not to mention their good humor.

"The streets of Viksfjord are filled with much peril," said Father. He stopped Torbjorn at the bottom of the gangplank and grasped him by both shoulders. "Go to find the money-clutching merchants in the village center. They will trade with you behind closed doors. Make your trade, then leave. Do not be seen. It's the Buttersmith's way."

It was the first time Torbjorn would bargain for himself, but Father didn't need to tell Torbjorn what to do. He'd seen the men come and go on trading trips dozens of times. And Torbjorn was a Smordaler through and through – it was in his blood.

"We don't want to attract attention," said Father, his yellow beard covering his belly like a thick blanket of hay. His mustache turned down at the corners – it meant that Father was frowning.

"I won't," said Torbjorn.

Torbjorn's 9-foot-tall brother Storfjell shoved past him. "Good luck, my brother," Storfjell said, punching Torbjorn in the arm. It nearly knocked Torbjorn off balance. "Do not settle for fish feet!"

I laugh my belly off, thought Torbjorn, frowning to himself. Fish feet were what you got when you'd been bamboozled. Torbjorn was not about to get bamboozled.

Torbjorn watched Storfjell chuckle as he ran up the beach into town. Storfjell was the only man 17 winters old who already had wrinkles growing out the corners of his eyes. His beard and mustache had turned silver early-on too. Father said it was because Storfjell had wisdom beyond his years. Sometimes Torbjorn wondered if that were really true. *More like stuffy beyond his years,* he thought.

Father also said Storfjell was his most responsible son. He counted on Storfjell to make reliable trades. Nothing extravagant or extraordinary, but Storfjell always brought back something useful for the clan. He was consistent, and that made Father happy.

When it came to Torbjorn, though, Father wasn't so go lucky. He was always telling Torbjorn to be a man, but Torbjorn already felt like one. He was 13 winters old! He already had a full red beard. He could do at least as well as Storfjell. Today, he was determined to do better.

Torbjorn threw his wool cloak over the basket of muffins. He paused as he passed a reddish bovine that had rowed alongside them. He patted her on the head – he so loved their bovines – then set out on the sand.

He passed a few small fishing boats, rounded an outcropping of rock, and found the wooden walkway that led into the village.

Viksfjord was big. Just from the shore, Torbjorn could see four separate, fortified enclosures, at least a few dozen lean-tos, a handful of ramshackle huts, and eleven wooden longhouses. There must have been a few hundred people living there, and even more stopping to trade. It was the biggest village Torbjorn had ever seen. Maybe the biggest village in all of the North. There was even a longhouse with carved dragon heads pointing out either end of its roof.

And then there were the streets: they were bustling with shoppers and merchants. There were people shouting from their doorways, people pushing carts. Torbjorn made his way carefully up into the swarm. This was the first time he'd gone into Viksfjord alone.

He shuffled between two barrels. The crowd made him nervous, especially when he had such important cargo.

"Cookies for your sweet tooth?" cried a bent old woman. She called out from behind a cart piled chin-high with sand-colored cookies. Stiff dark worms poked out of the tops and sides of the cookies like dried noodles. Torbjorn wrinkled his nose. She must have baked the worms into the batter. He could only imagine how ghastly that would taste.

Four boys half Torbjorn's age shoved past Torbjorn and jumped in front of her, waving tin coins at the woman. A tall man with a big mustache standing behind them chomped down on one of the cookies. Bits of gravel fell from behind his mustache. He made a face, picked a dried worm from between his teeth and spat.

He looked like he might throw up. Torbjorn couldn't blame him. It was times like this that reminded Torbjorn how lucky he was to have grown up in Smordal, where they'd perfected the art of muffin baking. Most clans were not known for making treats, and Torbjorn did not have to eat worms to know how rotten those clans' baked goods were.

Torbjorn squeezed his basket past the cookie cart. He dodged a man hauling a stack of wooden shields, turned around, and came face-to-face with two giant whale fins flopped over a pile of smoldering coals.

The shiny black fins were still attached to a humongous whale's tail. The coal bed was chest high to a sweaty man with a gap in his teeth who was fanning the flames with a dirty shirt.

"Would you like a taste?" the sweaty man asked Torbjorn. He cut off a long, stringy slice and dangled it from his finger. It smelled like fish rotting in hot candle wax.

"It's meaty," he panted through the gap in his teeth. He looked like he might faint.

"Nay," said Torbjorn. He batted away a fly and buried his nose in the fur on his shoulder to stifle the smell. He'd never seen anything so disgusting in his life.

"I got lucky. Ran over it with my boat," grinned the sweaty whale-roaster.

"Fortune shines on you," said Torbjorn, backing away as quickly as he could. He almost knocked over a man selling frozen bear paws on sticks, then turned around and sidestepped a boy with a muddy yellow toad clamped between two slices of brown bread.

The boy held the toad sandwich up to his wide open mouth and chomped down on it. The toad wriggled out in the nick of time, its feet squirming as it plopped down into the mud.

"My snack!" shouted the boy. He dove for the toad.

Torbjorn tried to maneuver past the boy, but it was too late. He tripped over the boy's leg, felt himself teeter, then scrambled to get his feet beneath him. His second foot caught behind his first and he toppled over onto the ground like a falling oak.

He slammed down hard in the mud, holding his precious basket of blueberry muffins aloft and absorbing the brunt of the crash with his chest. He gasped for air and tightened his stomach.

The cloak covering his basket flipped upward and a single blueberry muffin bounced out, rolled across the ground and stopped right in front of three hefty barbarians in muddy fur clothes.

The crowd suddenly, as if time had frozen, went silent. Torbjorn could see puffs of their breath hang in the air.

The tallest of the three barbarians looked down at the muffin and then back up at Torbjorn. He sniffed. Torbjorn could smell the buttery blueberry batter baked into bliss even from where he lay. Torbjorn had made a terrible mistake.

"Er?" said the tall Viking, when his two companions, an old hag, a pair of children and a cat all dove onto the muffin at once.

"A muffin trader!" someone shouted.

"BATTLE!" cried another. Suddenly, the woman standing next to Torbjorn smashed her fist into the face of the man behind her. He fell to the ground in a heap.

The resulting melee spread like an avalanche through the crowd. Knuckles crunching jaws, carts overturned, tunics torn asunder.

The sweaty whale roaster dove, arms and legs spread, on his whale tail. "My sea princess!" he cried. The boys with the tin coins dodged backward. One of them hooked the cloak covering Torbjorn's muffins on his boot. He kicked, and Torbjorn tried desperately to pin the cloak down before it tore free.

He managed in part, and for one full second that seemed like an eon, the muffins were left bare for all to see. Torbjorn wrenched the cloak free and wrapped it tight around the basket. Had they seen?

So far, he'd been lucky. He had to get away before anyone noticed that his basket was full of not just one, but a *mound* of blueberry muffins.

There was a crunch and a cry, then a whack, and the people-pile immediately on top of the single loose muffin toppled over as more Vikings dove to join it.

Torbjorn picked himself up off the ground and clutched the basket close.

He stepped over an old hag who was pulling the tail of a swine that had a skinny man's foot in its mouth. The man's arm was inside the pileup, no doubt feeling around for the escaped muffin. Torbjorn ducked a wooden bench heaved at his head and sidestepped a pair of Vikings yanking on each other's horned helmets. The bench smashed into the whale tail and knocked over the sweaty whale-roaster and the pile of coals, scattering them across the ground. The brawlers leapt and danced, their feet burning hot every time they touched the ground.

Torbjorn ducked around the corner of the nearest wooden house, shimmied his way into the narrow space between two buildings, and escaped out the other side, his basket of muffins still intact and his ribs still aching from his fall.

He was pretty sure no one had seen him, so he paused to catch his breath.

The second street was quiet, almost solemn by comparison. Grey mists rose up out of the ground, so that the colors in the village almost seemed quiet too.

Most towns had only one main street going down the middle. Viksfjord had several. It was the largest village Torbjorn had ever been to. To the right, the street extended the length of more than a dozen longboats. To the left it was twice as far to the end of the village, and Torbjorn could see the smoke rising gently beyond the wall made of pointed timbers in the distance.

He wondered if Storfjell and the rest of his clansmen had fared better than he had on the first street – they'd probably slipped past the brawlers unnoticed and gotten their goods into the hands of the seafaring merchants who could pay for them.

Once those merchants had gotten a basketful, they would sell the muffins in the market there. Others would set sail for far-off places, following trade routes south in either direction to other merchant towns where the muffins would fetch a higher price as exotic baked goods. Some would even make it as far as the lands where the sun stayed out in the winter. There the muffins would be honored in the banquet halls of kings.

In return, the merchants would pay generously, and Torbjorn's clan would sail back to Smordal, their ship laden with grain, cloth, and metal and wooden tools. It would take several trips to Viksfjord during the bright summer to gather enough food and supplies for

Smordal to survive the coming cold. Torbjorn was just lucky that he'd made it through the brawl with the muffins intact. He could only imagine what Father would say if he had lost the basket.

"You were clever to flee," said a man over Torbjorn's shoulder into his ear. Torbjorn turned. He'd thought he was alone.

The top of the man's head came to Torbjorn's chest. He was dressed in a grey cape, with a silver clasp pinned to his shoulder to fasten it in place. He wore leather shoes, something that few people back in Smordal could afford. He wore a long tunic underneath that hung down to his knees, much like Torbjorn's own. But his was woven of cloth the color of the setting sun or blood, something Torbjorn had never seen before. It was plain to Torbjorn that this man had money.

"A mouse does not like to stay when the dogs are hungry," said Torbjorn.

The man nodded. "Well spoken. I am Rotte the Righteous," said the man, bowing his head slightly and lifting one edge of his cape outward. His face was older and pleasant, his nose large, with a wide, warm smile underneath it – a face that seemed clever in its own right.

Torbjorn returned the greeting with a slight bow.

There was a shout from the crowd at the other side of the houses.

"Come," said Rotte, and beckoned Torbjorn down the lane. "They will be looking for the owner of the muffins. I have a place you can come indoors," he said.

Torbjorn followed Rotte. He was probably right. It was best to lie low for a few moments until the village settled down and Torbjorn could go out again.

Besides, if he were as wealthy as he looked, Rotte might be able to pay handsomely for the muffins himself.

Rotte led Torbjorn to a wooden lodge that was smaller than the rest and stopped at the door. Torbjorn hadn't seen this lodge before. It was made of planks fitted closely together, with a sloping wooden roof covered in dying grass. But it was not the lodge itself that caught Torbjorn's eye. In the center of a flat door carved with looping branches was a single, hideous, curled stone finger.

The finger was as large as Torbjorn's hand, gnarled and bony, with a thick, split fingernail that had grown to a claw on the end. There was a wart on the third knuckle, and fine wrinkles carved across the skin. Torbjorn had never seen a carving so intricate or lifelike. It was almost as if it were a real finger covered in stone.

"Troll's finger," said Rotte.

"Very fine workmanship," said Torbjorn.

"A carving of course. Everyone knows trolls died out hundreds of years ago," Rotte chuckled warmly.

"Is it true, that they could not cross water?" asked Torbjorn. He'd heard the lore told around the fire.

"That's what has been said, but I cannot say," smiled Rotte. There was something in the way that Rotte's lips curled inward that made Torbjorn wonder if he wasn't telling the whole story.

"I see it interests you," said Rotte, opening the door. "There are more of such things inside, if that is your wish," Rotte said.

Torbjorn did want to see what was inside. The troll's finger was a treasure in itself. And Rotte did seem so kind.

"Come," said Rotte, and pushed the door inward. He beckoned to Torbjorn. "I have untold wonders for the curious."

Torbjorn could not resist. He stepped down into the lodge, squeezing his basket of muffins between the door posts. He absolutely had to know what was inside.

Chapter 3 — The Sword of Weyland

The lodge was dark, except for the fire smoldering on the hearth in the middle of the floor. The walls were decorated with wooden shields painted in bright colors like the sky and the trees. The beams supporting the roof were carved like the door – curls intertwined with snakes. At the crossbeams was a large wolf with its jaws open wide.

The floor was made of planks of wood too, like the deck of Torbjorn's clan's ship. Most shops had only dirt floors – certainly nothing back at home in Smordal was so fine. It meant that Rotte was definitely rich.

A long table against the back wall confirmed Torbjorn's suspicion. It was piled with stamped silver coins and a bowl of green glass beads. They were probably from far away in the east and worth enough to buy an entire herd of sheep. It meant that Rotte the Righteous could pay handsomely for the muffins, if Torbjorn could convince him to trade for them.

"Tell me," said Rotte the Righteous as he ushered Torbjorn to a bench, "what is it about the butter on your muffins that makes them taste as if they came from kings?"

So this man, besides being rich, was clever. Torbjorn wasn't sure how to answer. Few merchants had ever guessed that the magic of the muffins lay in the layer of butter smeared across the top. They did not know that was what preserved their freshness and taste. They did not know that even more than making blueberry muffins, the people of Smordal were Buttersmiths.

Rotte the Righteous knew their secret – it put Torbjorn at a disadvantage. He felt disarmed. And now Rotte was asking Torbjorn to tell him more.

"I do not know but that our muffins are baked with centuries of wisdom from our clan," said Torbjorn.

"You come from Smordal, do you not?" asked Rotte.

Torbjorn nodded. Rotte knew that too.

"The hidden valley, which they say is cradled by mountains and watched over by the moon?"

Indeed, that is what they say, Torbjorn thought. Rotte knew far too much. Smordal's whereabouts were not something they spoke of to others. They kept to themselves for the most part, living in their hidden valley at the end of a narrow fjord. They only left to trade, and never brought visitors there. Father said that is what kept them safe.

Rotte already knew so much; what could Torbjorn tell him that he had not already discovered? He had to win the man's trust to make a good trade. He would have to confide in him to do that. But if he told Rotte more than Rotte already knew, he'd reveal their secrets. So he just nodded, hoping to buy some time.

"Please, rest yourself," Rotte said, gesturing to a bench next to the table. Torbjorn hesitated, then sat down. He did not want to be rude. Besides, it would give him a chance to set down the burden in his arms. He heaved the basket of muffins onto the table.

Rotte peeled back the cloak and plucked a muffin from the pile. He held it close to his nose, sucking in the aroma. "You cannot hide their true worth from me," he said, smiling. "I could smell their golden coating before I even saw your face."

Torbjorn looked to the door.

"You mustn't worry," said Rotte. "I am your friend."

He pulled a long object wrapped in a cloth from a shelf on the wall. He laid it on the table and unwrapped it. Inside was an iron sword. "Now, I will tell you a secret of mine in return."

"This iron comes from Trollstigen, the troll's stairway. It was hewn out of the rock there," he said. He handed the sword to Torbjorn.

Torbjorn took it by the hilt in one hand and laid the flat end of the blade on his other palm. It was magnificent. The hilt was sturdy and carved with a light pattern for grip. The blade was straight. The edge was even steel. A sword like this would be an excellent prize for Father. They weren't warriors in Smordal, but such a sword could help in defense. It would command respect from their enemies. "It is remarkable," said Torbjorn.

"It was forged by Weyland the Smith himself," said Rotte.

Torbjorn looked at him to see if he was telling the truth. Torbjorn had heard stories of Weyland. He was a blacksmith so skilled at forging swords, they say he even forged the sword that Odin himself stuck in the tree Barnstokkr. Torbjorn had thought Weyland was just a legend. "This is a fine sword, but that cannot be!" said Torbjorn.

"Who else could have forged it?" smiled Rotte. He snatched the sword from Torbjorn's hands. Torbjorn jumped back, and Rotte swung the blade high in the air, then brought it down like a hammer on an iron poker that stuck out of the fire. The sword cut the poker cleanly in two.

Torbjorn gasped. He'd never seen a sword do such a thing. If not Weyland the Smith, then who? Its blade gleamed, even in the low firelight of the house.

"It could be yours," Rotte said.

So, he did want to trade. "Half of the butter-covered golden muffins," Torbjorn stammered. "Blueberries included." He knew the sword was worth five basketfuls at least, if not twice that, but Father had taught him to negotiate.

Rotte smiled. "You know I cannot accept that offer," he said, shaking his head.

"The full basket then," said Torbjorn. He did not want to offend his host. Most of all, he did not want to lose a sword forged by Weyland the Smith.

Rotte frowned. "No, friend. I want something much less in return. I will not take your sacred golden blueberry muffins from you. Instead, all I ask is that you satisfy my curiosity."

Torbjorn frowned. He did not understand.

"I have told you my secret. And now, all I wonder is if you can tell me what it is that makes your butter sing songs and tell tales to the tongue, that all who taste it want more?"

It was a strange request. Torbjorn knew that the butter of Smordal was the envy of all clans – without those clans even knowing that's what made their muffins taste so good. But he'd supposed it was the fact that they'd only fed their bovines on fresh green clover, or that they'd treated the herd like family. Or perhaps it was the sunshine of Smordal, or the sparkling streams that fed the fields. Or the women churned the milk into cream and sang as it thickened into golden butter. It was all of these things that turned butter into gold, but not just one of them. It was not something he was sure he could explain in an afternoon, or even perhaps a lifetime. Then he realized for the first time that it was not something he knew.

"Our streams perhaps? Or the green crisp clover which the bovines eat," he said.

"Many clans have these things," said Rotte.

Torbjorn shook his head. "Then I cannot say," he said.

Rotte frowned. His eyebrows pushed together and his face turned sour. "Not because you do not know, but because you will not tell!" he shouted. He whisked the sword away, wrapped it back in its cloth, and shoved it onto a shelf, out of sight.

Torbjorn was shocked. He had not expected someone who'd seemed so calm to make such an outburst.

"I had trusted you, and now you give me nothing in return!" said Rotte. There was anger in his words. He stomped to the door and threw it open. "Be gone," he said, pointing out toward the water's edge.

How quickly Rotte had lost his temper! Torbjorn did not know what to do. He hadn't meant to insult him. He wished right then that Father were there. Or even Storfjell. Father would know what to say.

But Father was not there, so Torbjorn hefted the basket of muffins. He wanted to do or say something to show Rotte he'd not meant him any dishonor. He plucked a muffin from the basket and placed it on the table. It seemed a pathetic gesture, once he'd done it, but one he could not take back now.

Rotte stepped aside to give Torbjorn plenty of space on his way out, as if he were disgusted to be in the same house. There was nothing more Torbjorn could do. He stepped out the door.

"I don't want it," said Rotte. The muffin came sailing out of the doorway and rolled into the street. The door slammed shut behind Torbjorn with a clap.

He had failed.

"You going to be eating that?" said a dirt-smudged boy half of Torbjorn's age. He was pointing at the muffin where it had come to a stop in the mud. Torbjorn shook his head. The boy scampered away, stuffing the muffin into his mouth as he went.

Torbjorn frowned at himself. He had missed a perfect opportunity. He should've tried to explain better how they churned their butter into gold. He wasn't sure how to describe it entirely – it's just what they did.

He'd never realized before that perhaps he did not entirely know. If that were the case, perhaps he wasn't really a Buttersmith at all. That left him feeling hollow, like maybe he didn't understand what it meant to be a part of the clan that he loved so much.

***

By the time Torbjorn had made his trades, it was getting late and the sun was dipping toward the horizon. It only disappeared for a few hours each night during the summertime, but the shops would be shutting down, and the men of his clan bedding down for the night on their ship. They would set sail early the next day. He headed toward the water again, his basket empty. He'd only managed to get some dried fish and a few sacks of grain. It was by no means a poor trade, but thoughts of Weyland's sword ran through Torbjorn's head as he climbed the plank back onto the ship. The sword would've been a wonderful gift to Father. It would've made him proud.

Someone stomped up the gangplank behind Torbjorn. There was a cheer from the men onboard. Torbjorn turned. It was Storfjell. He held a sheep under his arm. "There will be wool, and one day meat!" cried Father. His hay-colored beard rustled at the corners again.

"Maybe even socks!" said another.

Storfjell beamed from ear to ear so bright, his silver beard shined like trout scales. "Or scarves! For the bovines!" he said, tossing the sheep to Father.

Torbjorn stepped aside, sliding to the back of the ship while everyone's attention was on Storfjell. Torbjorn's feeling of hollowness grew inside him. Storfjell once again had proved himself the responsible one.

Torbjorn shoved his grain sacks and dried fish to the side of the deck. He slunk down on them, hoping he wouldn't be noticed.

He had failed. It wasn't just Storfjell's sheep, or that Torbjorn had lost the sword. It was something else. Torbjorn loved Smordal and loved being a part of his clan more than anything. The thing that bothered him most was that for the first time he began to wonder if he really knew what it meant to be a Buttersmith at all.

Chapter 4 — The Nine Churns

As the evening fell, Torbjorn's mind grappled with a single thought. Ever since Rotte the Righteous had mentioned it, Torbjorn wondered about it, and now that it was late, and he had settled on the deck of the ship with a bag of grain for a pillow, he resolved to ask Father the truth.

The men of Smordal were dozing and humming as the evening finally grew grey – not fully dark, but the grey of a Northern summer night. "Father," said Torbjorn, "I know our herd of bovines has been the finest for generations, and I know that they eat only the fresh clover that is fed by mountain streams, and I know that the sun shines on our valley of Smordal at just the right angle all summer long, but which of all these things turns our butter into gold?"

Father sat up from the deck and rested his arm on his knee. He was respected by the clan for his wisdom, perhaps even as much as Smordal's Chief Gradfir himself. He sighed a long, heavy sigh and said, "When each boy comes of age, we tell him the tale, like my father told me, and his father told him. It is the secret of the clan. It is the means by which Buttersmiths turn butter to gold. Wake your brother."

Torbjorn did as he was told, and thumped Storfjell on the head with his fist. Storfjell bolted upright, yawned, and thumped Torbjorn back. Torbjorn fell over. "Time for breakfast?" Storfjell yawned.

"Nay," said Father. "It is time for the lore of the Smordaler, which will not fill your belly, but your heart with wisdom."

Father's voice became deep and distant: "All these things you say of our butter are true, Torbjorn Trofastsonn, but there is one thing yet which you must know – that is the thing that above all else turns our butter into gold."

Torbjorn felt his heart quicken. This was the thing he must know.

"You know, my sons, that men age, and grow grey. So it is with the gods and even Odin himself: they too would grow old if it were not for shining apples that grow on a tree in the midst of Asgard, the home of the gods. Every day the goddess Iduna plucks the shining apples from the tree and gives them to the gods to eat. Every day when they eat the apples their immortality is renewed, and they remain young and strong. The apples give them their power and their strength. If it were not so, they could not rule in Asgard and watch over men.

"Once long ago in our blessed valley of Smordal, where the moon shines fairly upon us, before our fathers had learned to turn butter into gold, there came a wanderer. He was tall, with a staff in hand, dressed in a grey cloak and wide-brimmed hat upon his head that hid his face. He had nearly perished for lack of food, and our fathers brought him into their longhouse and warmed him, and gave him bread to eat.

"When he was satisfied, he turned back his cloak and hat, and revealed that he was a one-eyed man of great strength. He gave our fathers a gift for their kindness, a single shining apple that was plucked from that very tree in Asgard which Iduna tends. He told us it would give strength and prosperity to our people if we used it in wisdom. And then he vanished.

"There were long councils held amongst the elders of Smordal to decide what they might do with the shining apple. Some argued that they should make a sauce so delicious, each clansmen would be satisfied with only one bite. Others argued for a pie, saying that it would please the gods. A third group said they must give it to their chief to eat, to give him youth. Others said that too would fade after time. Finally, the chief in his wisdom decided the apple's fate. He took the shining apple and planted it in the earth in Smordal, where the sparkling streams could feed it. The apple sprouted from the ground and grew into a stout and beautiful tree. The sun shined in Smordal and kissed the leaves of this tree and the clan waited for the tree to bear its fruit. And they rejoiced in the wisdom of their chief, for now they would have shining apples in abundance until the end of their days.

"In this they were disappointed, for Iduna's tree cannot bear fruit in Midgard, the home of men, like it had in Asgard, the home of gods.

"The chief counseled wisely once again, and commanded them to cut the tree down, and from it, the people of Smordal carved nine wooden churns with which to churn their bovines' milk into creamy golden butter. And those are the churns that we in Smordal use today, cut from a tree that grew from the shining apple of Asgard. The Nine Churns give our butter its magic taste, and turn the life-milk of our bovines into gold."

Torbjorn shifted to his knees. He had seen the churns hundreds of times. The women of the village used them to churn the milk of the herd into delicious, creamy butter. He had watched his mother spend hour upon hour pushing the wooden handle up and down inside the barrel-like chamber to stir the milk until it became thick and creamy. There were nine of them, each one carved with runes spiraling around its width and up its handle. He'd never seen such skilled woodwork, even in Viksfjord.

Torbjorn had never been allowed to touch the churns himself. The clan held the churns in such high regard that they protected them like children. They passed them down from generation to generation. Now he understood why.

"And such it is, my sons. When you are men soon, you will guard the Nine Churns that are the children of the tree which grew from Asgard's shining apple," said Father.

Torbjorn laid his head on the sack of grain again and looked up into the stars that had just come into the sky. He did not know what to think of the lore his Father told. It was wonderful lore, and Father always told the truth, but this – this was beyond something he could imagine.

He looked to Storfjell, who stared solemnly at Father, as if absorbing the story as it lingered in the night. "And this is why we are Smordaler," said Storfjell. "The Buttersmiths."

In many ways, it made sense. Merchants and clans everywhere did seek the butter of Smordal. This would explain why it was so unique. *The pride of our clan*, thought Torbjorn, and drifted off to sleep.

Perhaps he would never tell Father about the sword he might have given him.

***

But he did tell Father about the sword forged by Weyland the Smith. It was brought to his memory a fortnight later, as they sailed back up the fjord into Viksfjord once again to make the final trade of the summer.

"A sword forged by Weyland would be a prize indeed," said Father as he tangled his fingers into the hay-colored beard on his chin. He shook his head. "But we are men of peace. Spears we keep, and shields we hold, but it is the secret valley of Smordal that protects us from raiders."

Torbjorn heaved a loaded basket of muffins on his back and stepped across the sand into the village. He deliberately turned left at the first road this time. He wanted to avoid the house at the end of the lane with the carved troll finger on the door. His failure there was still fresh in his mind, and he was determined to trade better this time. To make Father proud.

He picked his way through the merchants and villagers, extra careful to hold his muffins close.

"My friend, the one I have wronged," said a scratchy voice in the crowd. Torbjorn turned. It was the man in the cape with the wide smile – Rotte the Righteous. He was bowing to Torbjorn.

"I?" said Torbjorn. His stomach tightened at the sight of him. He and Rotte the Righteous had parted as enemies. He had embarrassed Torbjorn.

"I was without hospitality when you were a guest in my house," said Rotte. "And for that I must repay you."

Torbjorn furrowed his brows. This was unexpected. He had hoped not to see Rotte again at all.

"I have no need of your sword," said Torbjorn.

If that surprised Rotte, he did not show it. "No, I do not wish to trade. I have a thing of great worth to show you – as recompense."

Torbjorn hesitated.

"It is here, on this side of the village," said Rotte. He swept his hand toward the end of the village opposite his house. "Please."

"Very well," said Torbjorn. He followed Rotte past the second wall. It didn't take long to reach the edge of Viksfjord. The valley was wide and flat for miles before it ran into the mountain range that guarded either side of the fjord.

Rotte swept his arms out wide toward a field where dozens upon dozens of furrows were dug into the earth in straight rows. Torbjorn had never seen such a vast field for planting. It would yield plenty of grain for baking bread or hay for feeding herds. Anyone with a field like that could harvest a bountiful crop indeed. His clan would never go hungry or fear for winter. "It is a fine field," said Torbjorn.

"Can I show you how it is made?" Rotte smiled.

"Please," said Torbjorn.

He took him to a lean-to lashed together with sticks on the edge of the field. There was a barrel underneath it with something tall wrapped in thick cloth. Rotte pulled back the edge of the cloth. There was a hoe inside. It had a long wooden handle with a sturdy curve to it, and an iron blade fixed firmly to the end. Rotte handed it to Torbjorn, who took it in his hands.

The wood seemed to grow around the iron, the fitting was so tight. The blade tapered from a thick slab to a sharp edge. It gleamed. Torbjorn swung it in the air. It was balanced in his hands, so that his swing was effortless, like the hoe was heaving itself for him; he was merely guiding it. He brought it hacking down into the earth, but instead of jarring him, the blade cut into the hard soil like the ground was soft mud.

It was fine hoe indeed.

Rotte smiled showing a wide row of teeth under his beak nose. "It too was forged by Weyland."

Torbjorn said nothing. That could be. He peered close at the metal. The edge *was* steel, just like the sword.

Rotte knelt under the lean-to and swept the dirt back with his hands. Buried underneath was a long wooden box. He pried open the lid. There was a large, long bundle inside. "It has brothers. Altogether they are a dozen in their family. Here are six of them," said Rotte.

We could double the size of our harvest with such treasures, thought Torbjorn. *We could survive the winters without hunger.*

He had to know where it came from. "How did you get these?" He wasn't sure he could ask; it was certainly a treasure beyond any he had seen.

Rotte hesitated. His wide smile disappeared, and his mouth narrowed like a slash in the earth. "It is not for me to tell."

Torbjorn felt stabbed, and suddenly afraid that he'd never know. "I will give you my full basket – the blueberry muffins of Smordal!" It was a slim hope. He took the basket off his shoulders and set it before Rotte.

Rotte laughed. "Perhaps we are not so different, you and I!" he said.

He speaks true, thought Torbjorn. Perhaps they weren't so different.

Rotte handed him the hoe. "For you," he said. "I ask nothing in return. These hoes were a gift from Njord, the god of merchants, who brought them here because he wished Viksfjord to prosper. It is our great secret, the life of our village."

Torbjorn thought of the shining apples and the tree that his ancestors cut down to make the butter churns. They weren't so different then either, Smordal and Viksfjord.

"We have been given gifts, both of us. Your gift is truly a remarkable one," Rotte said. He eyed the basket of butter-covered blueberry muffins that was now between them.

"It is," said Torbjorn. Rotte had been generous with his secret. Torbjorn wanted to repay him somehow. He had something close to his own heart he wished to say. "Our butter churns as well came from the gods."

Rotte smiled a slow smile. "Oh?" he whispered. He put his fingertips together.

Suddenly Torbjorn realized what he had done. A heat welled up in his gut and rose to his neck. He'd been too quick. He'd said too much.

"You are not a man who needs swords, when tools can serve you best," said Rotte. "Here, take these as a gift." Rotte bent and pulled the bundle of Weyland's hoes from the box and held them out to Torbjorn with both arms. "Since we are as friends who share secrets."

Torbjorn hesitated. What was done was done. There was no taking back his words now. How he wished he could! He wanted to run. He wanted this moment to vanish.

Rotte must have felt his reluctance. "Do you not wish for this gift?"

What would he tell the clan when he returned with the hoes? How would he explain where they came from? "Take these," he nearly shouted. He took the basket from his back and shoved the blueberry muffins at Rotte, knocking the hoes to the ground. At the very least he could complete the trade. He gathered the bundle under both arms and ran back toward the ship.

When he saw it, he slowed. At least it would seem to the others that he'd made a fair trade, but in Torbjorn's heart he feared that he'd given up the greater treasure.

Chapter 5 — The Blodkriger

Out of the hundreds of fjords along the wrinkled, gnarled coast of the North, the fjord that led to Smordal was the least likely of all to hide a village. In fact, it was so unlikely that some seafarer might have noticed how unlikely it was, if not for the fact that it looked just likely enough. And that was just what kept Smordal hidden for so many centuries.

Father and the clan could not stop talking about the hoes when they sailed into the narrow fjord that led to Smordal. "We will have twice the harvest!" laughed Father.

"And half the back pains," shouted Mannkraft the Strong. There was an avalanche of laughter. Mannkraft was the mightiest of their clan, and perhaps the happiest about the hoes. He had dug more furrows than anyone. The hoes would make it easier for him to break the frosty ground come spring. "Perhaps I shall take up knitting with my extra time!" he shouted. They laughed again.

Torbjorn did not laugh with them. He sulked near the stern of the ship, staring back to sea from where they'd sailed. He should not have gone into town. He should have stayed at home. He had given up their greatest secret to a treacherous stranger. He was certain nothing would come of it, but with everyone's excitement, it was hard to shove it out of his memory. Their jolliness somehow made things worse.

"Torbjorn, the shrewd trader! Come, man the oars with us!" called Mannkraft the Strong.

That is when Torbjorn spotted the other ship.

It was far off on the horizon, at the very edge of the fjord. It was smaller than the Smordal ship. It probably held no more than two dozen men, so it was lighter and faster in the water too.

"What is that?" asked Storfjell, pointing to the ship. He dropped his oars onto the deck and left them to look. "Look! Look at its sail!" There was fear in his voice.

Torbjorn peered harder. Then he saw it too – on the sail was painted a wolf with open jaws – much like the symbol he'd seen carved in the crossbeams at Rotte the Righteous's house.

Torbjorn's heart sank. There was no denying it: Rotte the Righteous had followed him here.

Father left his oar and leapt to the back of the ship. He grasped the railing and leaned out so far over the water, it looked like he might fall in. "The Blodkrig Clan!" he cried.

The men shifted and shouted at the oars. The bovines stamped their feet. Mannkraft drew a spear from beside the mast and pounded its butt on the deck.

Torbjorn had not heard of the Blodkriger, but he did not have to ask to know they were dangerous. From the stir the ship caused with the men, he could guess what the Blodkriger wanted: they were here to raid Smordal.

"We must row with haste!" cried Mannkraft. "We must return and prepare our defense for our wives and children!"

Father nodded. "There is little time!" he said.

31

Torbjorn had never seen war before. It made him afraid. No one knew how a battle would end, what would be destroyed, who would suffer. He thought of his two sisters and his mother.

The men pushed the bovines aside and took hold of the oars. Father began to beat the drum near the mast. The men rowed furiously in time with his beats, heaving the oars as they dipped them into the water, pulling with their whole backs. The boat surged forward with each stroke.

Torbjorn took up an oar and rowed with them. He rowed until the sweat poured out of his helmet and into his eyes. He rowed until his hands were hot on the wood. He rowed as if somehow, by rowing, he could drive away the fear. This was the only thing he could do.

Drum. Drum. Drum.

They still had a long way to go before they reached the shore. The fjord leading into Smordal was several miles long, and sails were no use here. There were two major bends in the fjord, and with the cliffs so high on either side, they would lose sight of the raiders' ship until it too passed the bend.

They rowed round the first bend and the Blodkrig ship disappeared from view behind the cliff. They were nearly to the second when the ship reappeared, sooner than expected. They were gaining on them.

"Row!" cried Father, beating the drums with more force. They rowed even more furiously than before.

They lost sight of the enemy ship again as they rounded the second bend.

Torbjorn's shoulders burned with pain and his back ached with each stroke. Even Storfjell gritted his teeth tightly.

Torbjorn glanced over his shoulder between strokes. *Smordal.* It somehow looked even lovelier and more tranquil than he remembered, nestled between the steep cliffs on either side, a field of crisp, green clover growing behind the small collection of wooden huts and houses. His clansmen were gathered on the shore, waiting to greet them. Mother and his sisters were there too.

"Raiders!" shouted Mannkraft toward the shore. There was a cry of alarm. The Smordaler scattered, several of them running back into their houses. *Wooden houses are little protection from raiders,* thought Torbjorn.

The boat scraped against the sand just as the enemy ship came into view again. The Smordaler had gained a small lead this time, perhaps because there were more of them to row, or because Father knew the best way to steer through the fjord. Whatever moments they had gained would give them precious time to prepare what meager defense they could.

The men leapt from the boat into the sea. Torbjorn followed after, landing up to his waist in the salty water. He slogged along with the rest of them as quickly as he could until he was out of the water and onto the sand.

Chief Gradfir strode from the doorway of the main longhouse, his helmet already on his head, his spear in hand. "Mothers, take your daughters behind the herd-house!" he shouted as he fastened a leather armor chest plate around his shoulders. Torbjorn had always respected Chief Gradfir, but even Gradfir had never seen battle before.

"Bring those bovines ashore!" ordered Chief Gradfir. Someone threw the gangplank over the side of the boat and the bovines stamped their way down it into the water and up onto the sand.

Mannkraft and the other men rushed passed Torbjorn and thundered up the sand toward the main longhouse. Moments later, half of them emerged with spears and shields. The rest came from the stables with nothing more than pitch forks and spades. They were not equipped for war in Smordal.

Torbjorn's two sisters cowered near the edge of the family hut. Their golden hair curled about their shoulders. *Gudrunn and Eldrid*, thought Torbjorn. He said a prayer in his heart for them. They were barely half his age. "Run!" he cried, and pointed toward the back of the village where the herds grazed. The fear in their eyes told Torbjorn that they understood. Mother came out of the hut, her long golden hair bobbing and fluttering as she darted to the girls, then back indoors and back out again carrying a basket and a knife.

"Torbjorn! Storfjell!" she cried. She looked worried. Father ran to them, and pointed in the direction of the fields.

"Hurry!" he said. He hugged them, lingering, holding them tighter than Torbjorn had seen him do before. This wasn't like the farewell Father gave every month when he sailed to trade. This was different – and that meant that Father, the man who'd always protected them, was afraid too.

Father let them go and pushed them toward the fields. Then he took a spear from inside the house and shoved it into Storfjell's hands.

Torbjorn knew what that meant. He and Storfjell would fight. It was for the honor of Smordal, and even more, for the right for his family to live. "Father, what weapon will I use?" He thought of the sword forged by Weyland that he'd left in Viksfjord.

Father turned to him and pressed his hands on Torbjorn's shoulders. "No weapon, son. You will not fight. You must run. Take your sisters."

"No!" Torbjorn cried. It did not make sense. They needed him. He was old enough to trade – he should be old enough to fight.

"Aren't I strong enough?" said Torbjorn. He knew how Father would have to answer. Torbjorn had already shown his great strength to the men while packing the boats and felling trees for lumber. Now his heart was begging him to take action. If that action was battle, then fight he must.

"Battle demands wisdom as your ally," said Father. "Without it your strength is as thunder without lightning."

Torbjorn opened his mouth to protest. "You must keep your sisters and mother safe," Father said, cutting him off. "They have come for our herds. Without them, we will starve. Protect them. That is your duty now."

Torbjorn gritted his teeth. He knew that the Blodkriger had come for something else. He was sure of that. But now was not the time to explain.

Storfjell hefted his spear. He never looked more like a man than he did right then – he was not the same brother he had always been; there was majesty that went with his grave expression as he looked to the shore. "Battle," said Father. Then he hefted his spear too and led Storfjell charging toward the beach.

The Blodkrig ship was nearing the shore. They only had moments before it reached land. Torbjorn turned and took his sisters by the hands, and led them up behind the stables, where he took a wooden spade under his arm – better to have some weapon than none at all when the enemy came. He threw off the timber that held the main herd in their paddock, and with a swat of his hand, sent the first trotting out into the clover. The rest followed, joining the bovines from the ship and stampeding alongside Torbjorn, his mother and his two sisters into the fields.

He turned back to see the raiders leaping from their boat onto the shore with drawn swords; there was a shrill cry, then a volley of arrows from their ship battered the village, smashing into the sides of the longhouse, their shafts driving deep into the wood.

Chapter 6 — Raid

The women and children fled, running alongside the bovines as Torbjorn led them up toward the foot of the cliffs at the farthest edge of the clover field. The mothers carried the youngest children on their backs.

He turned for a moment. He could see movement in the village below, flashes of swords and the blur of shields, like a collision of insects, but he was too far to tell who'd gained the upper hand. It was strange, because out of earshot and so far away the battle below seemed slow, almost gentle, like walking men who were half asleep, or falling leaves drifting on the wind. It was like watching a bad dream.

I should be there, thought Torbjorn. *I could save them.* But Father and Storfjell were fighting just beyond his reach. It wasn't fair. He knew his strength. He could help them if they'd let him. He was certain of it.

Then the main longhouse's roof caught on fire. The blaze glowed in the fall's waning sun.

That could only mean that the battle had turned for the worse. There were shouts.

"Take the herd and gather them at the back of the valley," he told a little boy. The boy nodded and ran off.

The field of clover tapered to a point as it rose to meet the base of the granite mountains. There the valley funneled into a narrow pass that led between the cliffs. The pass split into several paths that twisted up the steep cliff face like jagged vines. For as long as Torbjorn could remember the clan had called those paths Farstigen, the Dangerous Climb.

Most of the women and children would gather at the narrow pass. Of all the men in the clover field, Torbjorn was the oldest. If their warriors failed, Torbjorn must lead what was left of the village up Farstigen to safety. He tried not to think about it. *They must conquer*, he thought.

And then, just as quickly as it had begun, the battle was over.

The Blodkrig ship began to drift slowly away from the shore. There were men scrambling to board it and more men pursuing them into the water. The oars came out, it changed course in a wide, clumsy arc, and gathered speed toward the mouth of the fjord and away from Smordal.

"Wait here," said Torbjorn to Mother and his two sisters. They did not protest. He ran down the valley past the stables to shore. He could not let himself take joy in victory just yet. The closer he came to the sand, the more he saw and the more he feared. It was a different fear than he'd had as the battle waged. Now that it was over, he was afraid to discover the depth of their loss. He wished he could be locked in the moment, never knowing what horrible things had already been finished.

There were men pouring seawater onto the roof of the longhouse to quench the flames. There were men lying on the sand, unmoving, next to broken spears that stuck out of the ground like splintered trees. There were men running back and forth to tend to their fallen clansmen. Torbjorn stood there, still as stone. It was all too much – smoke and blood and ruin – when Mannkraft seized Torbjorn by the shoulders. "Quench the flames!" he cried, thrusting a wooden bucket at Torbjorn.

He did not need to ask what Mannkraft meant. The longhouse. He shook himself, then ran to the water's edge, stepping over a fallen enemy who lay face-down in the sand. He filled his bucket with seawater and ran it back to the longhouse, where he sloshed it on the flames.

The flames swallowed the water easily. So he did it again. The second bucketful seemed to temper the fire just a little, steam rising up where the flames had been. He ran again, back and forth with the other men, all working as quickly as they could to fight the fire. The harder he worked, the less he had to face his thoughts: where was Father? Where was Storfjell?

There was no time to answer that now. He had to put the fire out. Then he'd find them. He threw another bucket. A few more, then the flames shrank, struggled, and went out.

They poured extra bucketfuls onto the roof until the wood was soaked through. The mist had been strong that month, so it had kept the wood and straw moist. Otherwise, there might not be a longhouse left at all.

Torbjorn dropped his bucket and slumped over against the outside of the walls to rest, the vapor from the sagging roof now floating away above the longhouse, like a memory of what the clan's gathering place used to be. The others stopped with him, all taking long hard breaths, when he heard a cry that pierced the moment.

On the beach was the body of Chief Gradfir, stretched out, lying face-up in the sand. One of the clan was kneeling over him, wailing.

Gradfir's armor had been knocked loose, so that it lay like an empty shell on the beach. His spear lay broken in two over his chest.

Gradfir, the mighty chief of their clan, the one without fear, the one who led them, had fallen.

Torbjorn took two careful steps toward him. The men rushed past Torbjorn to their chief. One of them knelt to inspect his wounds.

Torbjorn did not go any closer. This was work for older men; for once, he was glad he was not yet fully grown.

Now no one was safe. *Storfjell! Father!* he thought in alarm. If Gradfir could fall, so could they. The battle had been bitter, and it had been real. He scanned the beach frantically. There were fallen men from both clans, but no sign of Father or Storfjell.

He raced around the longhouse, and came to a span of open ground between two huts. "Father!" he called. He tried not to think of what might have happened. He tried to block the fear and loss from creeping into his chest. Instead, he replaced them with speed.

"Father!" he cried, racing to the sea side of the village again.

"I am here," said Father. He trudged out from behind a pile of hay, Storfjell hanging limply from his shoulder. An arrow stuck out of Storfjell's left forearm.

"Brother!" cried Torbjorn. Storfjell moaned, and a burst of hope lit in Torbjorn's chest.

"It is an arm wound," said Father. "I wish I had armor for my son, for he stood strong like a great mountain today."

Storfjell managed to grit a tight smile, showing a wide row of teeth like polished rocks.

"Mother can heal him," said Father, "But first we must pull the arrow from his arm."

There was confidence in Father's voice. Father set Storfjell against the longhouse, and braced Storfjell's arm underneath his knees. He pressed the arm flesh on either side of the shaft, then twisted the arrow slightly.

Mother brought a bucket of fresh water. She felt the wound. "It did not pierce his vitals," she said.

"The head is smooth. I will pull," said Father. He grasped the shaft firmly, the top of his closed fist facing down toward Storfjell's arm. Then he pulled steady and smooth. Storfjell kept his eyes clamped shut. Torbjorn could not tell if he was awake. Then Storfjell groaned so hard it shook the rafters of the longhouse.

The arrow came out of Storfjell's arm, and Father threw it to the ground.

Mother poured the water on the wound and bandaged it with a clean white cloth. She was crying. "My son!" she sobbed. Storfjell moaned again, then his head fell back, faint.

"He is strong, like the mountain," said Father. "He will rest, then he will eat, and he will live."

Torbjorn pressed the palm of his hand against his brother's chest and hoped that it would be true.

That night they gave Gradfir a hero's departure, smearing a skiff with golden butter and setting the brave Gradfir on board with his weapons and a small carved wooden bovine. Then they lit the butter; it blazed and burned as they sent the skiff drifting out into the fjord. No one wept, for they were Vikings; their hearts sang a sad song of praise. The burning butter lingered in Torbjorn's nostrils as he watched the skiff sink into the water. Torbjorn had always heard stories of war, but never had he seen it – nor had Father – and he wondered if he would forever be broken inside because of it.

Chapter 7 — Nectar of Moo

Storfjell did live. He woke that night after Gradfir's ceremony and sipped some onion soup. "Next time I shall block more of the arrows with my other arm so they don't break the longhouse," Storfjell grinned. Torbjorn did not think it was so funny.

"Then we can save what you have caught to shoot back at them," Torbjorn replied.

"I would rather that they shot sausages with their bows," said Storfjell.

Torbjorn almost laughed, because he too loved to eat sausages very much. It made him hungry.

And suddenly, Torbjorn smiled again. If Storfjell was no longer afraid, then maybe Torbjorn did not have to be either. Terrible things had happened when he'd given up Smordal's secret. But that was over now. There would be no need to speak of it again.

Besides, they had won. Smordal had proven itself in battle! They were warriors now. Without even a single sword, they had defeated the fierce Blodkrig Clan. Who else could Smordal defeat? Perhaps they were as strong as any clan north of Viksfjord.

That night, the men gathered in what was left of the longhouse and declared Father, Trofast Smakkersonn, the wisest of their clan, to be their chief. They pledged their loyalty and strength to Smordal and set a wreath of leaves on his head.

Mother opened a wooden box at the back of the longhouse. Inside were dozens of freshly sharpened horns. They all unscrewed the horns from their helmets and replaced them with the new ones in honor of their victory.

"Feast!" cried Mannkraft the Strong. He banged a mug against the long table next to the fire pit in the middle of the longhouse. "Yah!" cried the clan, and the feasting began.

This was not a feast like the puny feasts the clans of Viksfjord had – half a trout head each – nor even like the pitiful, meager feasts – three wilted leaves on a plate – of the clans of the East. This was a feast of Smordal, and there was never a feast that was more likely to put fat on your teeth than this one.

They piled the table chin-high with meats and cheeses from the storehouse and pears they'd brought from Viksfjord, and fish they'd caught from the sea. On top of that was a mound of blueberry muffins as high as a grizzly bear's back, all slathered in buttery gold.

Mother had even carved an exquisite, life-sized sculpture of Father out of a block of solid butter. She set it shimmering like gold atop the table, standing victorious with spear in hand. She'd even taken the time to carve hairs in his beard and pupils into his eyes. No one was more proud of Father tonight than she was. The butter chief was so real, Torbjorn thought that Father himself might be hiding inside.

"Hail to our Chief!" bellowed Mannkraft, opening the doors to the longhouse. "Mooverk, bring in the bovines!"

Mooverk was a small, nervous man with only a wisp of hair left on his balding crown. He spent most of his time tending the herd. He'd stayed in the stable when the attack came. Now, he ushered the herd into the longhouse through the doors. There were brown ones and reddish ones and white ones with spots, all streaming into the house and lining up at the table's edge, shoulder to shoulder, flicking their tails and smiling with their eyes, just like well-behaved bovines do. Mooverk pulled the first in line up onto the table until she was standing with her hooves next to the meats, her udder at eye level. He squeezed her teats, squirting warm, frothy milk into a mug. "Let us drink the Nectar of Moo!" Mannkraft said, sliding the mug down the table between the meats and cheeses until it landed in Storfjell's hands.

"Yah!" they shouted, banging the table in unison. Mooverk led the next bovine in line up onto the table and milked her too until she was all empty. Then he moved on to the next, Mannkraft sliding milk-mugs to everyone in turn. They drank sweet Nectar of Moo until a foamy white milk mustache covered each one of their upper lips – even Mother's. Nothing tasted so good to Torbjorn in all of the North. This was what it meant to be from Smordal.

And then the singing began. The men began swaying their milk mugs in time, their voices bouncing up and down, belting out such ancient traditional songs as "Loki's Got My Pajamas" and "Battle Axe in B Minor."

Torbjorn hadn't felt so happy in days. He was so busy catching the sausages that Mannkraft threw across the room into his mouth that he almost didn't notice Father quietly slip out the back and into the night.

***

Three days later, the men lay languidly on the benches and floor of the longhouse, picking at bits of muffins and dozing between sausages. Torbjorn did not know if he could bear to hear "Thor's Hammer Lost its Nails" one more time.

Mannkraft did not join them. Instead, he sat in the corner sharpening his spear. Storfjell also sat aloof away from the fire, stroking his mustache.

"Did you see us in battle?" cried Mooverk, his skinny arms waving back and forth.

"Yah!" cried Grimbarn, Mannkraft's son. "With warriors like ours, we could storm Viksfjord and take it for ourselves!"

The men laughed so loud, they sounded like a flock of geese eaten by a grizzly bear, when suddenly Father rose from his bench in the corner.

"Enough!" Father struck the table loudly with the butt of his spear. It shook the wooden bowls and in an instant, the songs ceased, and the men were still.

Torbjorn had not seen Father come in. Now that he was there, the fire light danced and shimmered on his hay-colored beard as he stood before them, his gaze piercing. Torbjorn did not dare to look him in the face.

"It's been three days," said Father. "Two days for the scouting party to travel to Viksfjord. Two more days to gather more soldiers and return. The Blodkriger will return, and this time in greater numbers."

"Tomorrow is the fourth day," whispered Mannkraft. He thumbed the edge of his spearhead.

Father nodded. "Our men are few, and our injuries are many," he said. "We cannot fight them again."

Torbjorn sat up. Why would the Blodkriger come back? Smordal had already won. He felt the joy in his chest darken.

"But we have little treasure! What could they want?" said Grimbarn.

"The fame of Smordal, the succulent blueberry jewels set in the crowns of our golden brown muffins!" cried Mother. She too had moved away from the feast to the edge of the longhouse.

One of the men laughed. "But they are just muffins!"

"That fetch a mighty price with kings!" replied Mother. Mother was not afraid of the men – as fierce as they were, they knew she was wise.

"They're after our herds!" cried Mooverk.

"Perhaps so," said Father. "We cannot know for certain what they seek, except for our destruction."

A thought formed in Torbjorn's mind and pounded against his throat, demanding to be spoken. He knew what they wanted. If he told them, he'd have to reveal his mistake. But if he didn't – the danger was real. "They seek the Golden Fortune of our Herds. They know our secret," he said.

Father nodded. "Of course. One cannot taste the blueberry muffins of Smordal season after season and not discover their savory secret. Time has been generous to us that this has not happened before."

Torbjorn felt a small sense of relief. Father had always tried to defend his son, but there was more for Torbjorn to say. He had to tell the whole truth. "In Viksfjord, the man who offered me Weyland's sword, I spoke to him of the Nine Churns." Torbjorn said, spitting out the words as fast as he could.

It was Mannkraft who roared first. "The Nine Churns that turn our bovines' nectar into gold? The churns fashioned from the tree grown from the shining apple of Asgard?"

"The very same," whispered Torbjorn.

Mannkraft pounded the table with his fist. "And now we have paid in blood!" There was a roar and shout from the men.

Torbjorn chanced a look up into Father's eyes. Father stared at him over the firelight, but his face betrayed neither pride nor shame.

Mother cried out. "You couldn't have known what it would bring upon us," she said.

The words stung, though Mother did not mean them to. She was right – Torbjorn could not have known it would come to this. But he had been foolish to lead Rotte and the Blodkriger here. He could not deny that.

"You fool," said Mannkraft, turning his back on him. There was a murmur of agreement.

"Enough," said Father. The men went quiet. "I will deal with my son later. Now we must speak of survival."

"We do not have the strength to fight them," said Mannkraft. "Look at our men – we have few left who can wield a spear, and even fewer weapons. We are not warriors!"

"Give them what they want!" cried Mooverk.

"Our churns?" cried Storfjell. "But that is what makes us Smordal! Without them we are nothing!"

Father spoke, "Better to give them the work of wood and iron than our own flesh and blood."

The words hung in the air. Torbjorn stared into the fire, listening as the sound of the clan's breath mingled with the crackling coals. Father was right.

"We must give them the Nine Churns. Then we must go up Farstigen, the winding cliffs to the forests. If we give them what they want, they won't follow us there," said Father. "Gather the herds. Gather bread, fish, and as many succulent muffins as we can take.

They will sustain us for a little while. We can only hope that somehow the forest will provide for us in such dark days as now."

Farstigen would not be easy for the entire village, plus the herd, to climb. Torbjorn had been up the paths once as a boy. They were steep and narrow. The herd and his family would have to walk single file to keep from falling off the edge. It would be dangerous. Especially for his sisters.

"We should gather the churns," whispered Mooverk. Father nodded.

All at once, there was a howling of wind, a trotting of hooves, as if four horses thundered down the valley all at once. The door to the longhouse flew open.

A tall grey stranger with a staff in hand stood there in the night. He wore a wide-brimmed grey hat that draped over his eyes and face, his cloak covering a majestic frame.

Chapter 8 — The Wanderer

"Hear me!" bellowed the stranger. His voice shook the walls; Torbjorn could feel it penetrate his ribs.

He leapt back off his bench and crouched low against the wall. If there was going to be a fight, he would be ready. The men lunged for their weapons; the stranger held up his hand and the fire surged hot and bright. "I bring no harm to you!" he said.

The men stepped back, covering their faces from the heat. It would be foolish to fight such a stranger. Someone who spoke to the flames could not be slain by spears alone. But if the other men attacked, Torbjorn would join them.

"I am Vegtam, the Wanderer," the stranger said. He was tall and thin. A black raven perched on each of his shoulders like two shadows, their eyes flickering and their feathers ruffling as they flexed their talons on his grey cloak. One of the Wanderer's eyes was missing. It was frightening the way his socket was scarred and empty where an eyeball should have been.

"This is not the first time I've come to Smordal. Your fathers' fathers knew me, and I brought them gifts. So too do I bring a gift to you tonight. The gift of foresight and knowledge."

Father held out his hands as if to hold the men back, but they were already settled, fidgeting nervously at the edge of the fire, listening to the Wanderer's words. The bovines stamped their hooves.

The two ravens fluttered from the stranger's shoulders over the fire, circling it and beating it with their wings. The flames dimmed and turned blue, then danced and swirled until they formed a tree. "Your fathers planted a shining apple in the ground. From it came the tree, and from its wood, the Nine Butter Churns imbued with the power of Asgard," the Wanderer said.

The tree fell and shattered to lumber. The pieces came together and formed the nine churns that Torbjorn had seen so often. The very same churns Mother sat at and worked with the fresh milk-nectar of the bovines.

So it *was* him – the Wanderer was the very same stranger Father had spoken of in the lore of the Smordaler.

"With the Nine Churns you spin the nectar of the bovines into gold. This is the envy of all of Asgard. You have not known when the Asgardians sought your muffins in the markets in secret, to taste just a hint of the golden butter for themselves. This is the Golden Fortune of your herds. You are the Buttersmiths. The Nine Churns are Asgard's gift to you, and the butter is your gift to all of Midgard."

Father dropped to his knees by the fireside. "Wise One," he said, "Our village is at stake. Our people face doom. We cannot fight the enemy again."

The folds beneath the Wanderer's good eye sagged. He was silent for a long time as he looked each man in the face. He almost looked sad. "I cannot interfere more than I already have," he whispered.

"But know this: the fruit of your churns must live. One day, because of its power, men will beat their swords into cooking pots, and the roar of the dragons will cease. It has a destiny beyond what battles you fight on the morrow. You cannot forsake the Nine Churns. It has been spoken!"

With that, the two black ravens flapped to him and landed on his shoulders. There was a rushing of wind, and a surge of the fire so hot and bright that Torbjorn had to cover his face and eyes.

When he looked again, the grey Wanderer was gone.

Chapter 9 — Plans

"He has spoken," whispered Father. Suddenly Father's ruddy face looked weary and old, like he'd been through seven more battles in a moment. It was the weight of worry that pulled down on his hefty cheeks.

"We will fight," said Mannkraft. "We will fight like dragons, and up in Asgard, they will know that they can lean on the furious spears of Smordal!"

Torbjorn traced his finger in the dirt at his feet. When Father had told him the legend of the Nine Churns, he'd believed it. The Wanderer had confirmed that it was all true, and Torbjorn had seen him with his own eyes now. But never had it occurred to Torbjorn that his clansmen would give their lives to protect the Nine Churns. He did not know if they could defeat their enemy; the battle had been severe. He wanted to hope that Smordal could triumph. They had for now. Tomorrow – Torbjorn just could not say.

But then… they were Smordal. And he was Torbjorn, the mighty son of Chief Trofast. Mannkraft had been the center of the battle before. If he was so certain, how could Torbjorn doubt? Torbjorn had been raised in the valley of Smordal, eating its golden butter since he was born. That surely had to count for something.

"The Blodkriger will learn to fear the men of Smordal," said Torbjorn.

"Yah," said the men in agreement. But there were no cheers or banging of spears this time. They almost sounded… afraid.

But Torbjorn was ready. *If they are not prepared, then this battle will rest on the courage of the few.*

Regardless of their fear, the choice had been made. There was no more counsel to take. The Wanderer from Asgard had spoken. Mannkraft took the spears and dealt them out to the men. He handed one to Torbjorn.

"He will not need it," said Father, taking the spear from Torbjorn's hand.

"But – " said Torbjorn. Now was not the time for Father to treat him like a child.

Father glared at him. "You must lead the people into the valley and up the winding paths of Farstigen."

"But you need warriors now more than ever!" said Torbjorn.

Father shook his head. He would not listen. The plan was set.

Torbjorn did not argue. This time, Torbjorn did not need Father to agree. He knew what he would do.

"Take the Nine Churns," said Father to Storfjell. "You must hide them up in the valley; if Fortune turns her back on us, and we are overcome, they will be safe. You must fight until your last breath for Smordal."

Storfjell did not reply. His silence could only mean one thing: resolve. It did not seem like warrior's work, but Storfjell took his spear and loaded the Nine Churns, carved and beautiful as daggers' handles, upright into a wagon. He pushed the wagon up into the valley where he could try to hide them in the mountains.

In a way it made sense that Storfjell should be the one to protect the churns. Torbjorn loved Smordal, but Storfjell loved it in a different way. He loved its past. He loved its lore. If Torbjorn loved the Smordal of today and tomorrow, Storfjell loved the Smordal of centuries gone by.

Torbjorn turned to prepare for departure. The nights had grown dark now that summer was over. They packed muffins and dried fish on the bovines' backs by candlelight, and once all the women and children were gathered together, they began the journey up through the clover field toward Farstigen.

Torbjorn let Mother and the other women and children pass him as they crossed the last of the green fields. Farstigen was the only way out of the valley besides the fjord. The path split off in several directions, like the branches of a tree, and was so narrow, Torbjorn remembered flattening himself up against the rock when he was young to keep himself from falling. If it weren't for the trips Torbjorn and the other boys had taken up the face, he wasn't sure he'd be able to navigate the maze to the top.

It took hours for the entire herd to make it onto the start of the path. Torbjorn watched as the last bovine followed the women and children onto the base of the cliff. She was a reddish brown heifer with brown, watery eyes. She stopped, stamping her hoof on the brittle grey stone at the end of the clover.

Maybe she sensed the danger. Maybe she even feared for the clan. Without thinking, Torbjorn suddenly clasped both of the bovine's cheeks with his broad hands, and kissed her on the forehead. "I will return for you," said Torbjorn.

And then Torbjorn turned and ran down through the spongy green clover back toward the village. He knew he was defying Father's wishes, but Mooverk was with the herd, and Mother too.

The women and children would know the way up the steep paths. Torbjorn was going to do what he was meant to do. He was going to fight.

He hid himself behind the smokehouse on the edge of the village. As the morning grew, and the grey light melted away and the colors of the rocks and trees and sky began to glow, he saw a faint smear of color emerge from around the bend in the fjord. Three red sails. Just like Father said they would, the Blodkriger had come.

Chapter 10 — Battle

The morning colors began to show themselves; Torbjorn could tell that men were not trees, but there was still not enough light to tell who was who. Two of his clansmen were crouched, their backs turned to him, waiting behind the boulders on the edge of the village near the last hut. They could probably see the battle better from there.

All he had was the same spade from before and a small knife that he kept on his belt. He so badly needed a spear.

Torbjorn started for the next closest hut, when he heard a whisper and a clatter of shields. Three more men – Smordaler – lay on the ground on the south side of the smokehouse. They were whispering frantically to one another. Torbjorn couldn't make out what they were saying, but their words were filled with dread.

So Torbjorn crouched low, and almost forgetting himself, crawled out from behind the smokehouse and fixed his eyes on the ships that were now easily in view.

He felt himself freeze with fear. This was it. This was real. Was it too late to run back up to Farstigen? That's not what he came for, he told himself. So he bit his lip and tried to concentrate on the moment. He was as strong as any of the men. He *would* prove it.

Of the three ships, one was closest to shore – just beyond an arrow's reach. It had stopped, drifting idly on the current, as if the rowers were waiting for something. It was a strange stance for their small fleet to take, and unless every one of their oars had broken, a foolish one that would allow the Smordaler an even greater advantage.

Then Torbjorn saw it – the reason they had stopped. They were making a show of their power. Now he understood the garbled word his clansmen spoke, and it filled him dread and disbelief: "Trolls."

This was no time for fairytales, but there was no mistake: chained to the deck, near the ship's pointed, upturned bow, was a monstrous, gnarled, hideous troll.

The troll must have been a head taller than Mannkraft. It was humongous, even from Torbjorn's distant vantage point. His shoulders were broad and bare, with a neckless head that was nothing more than a large bump on the top of his chest. His skin was the color of rocks – all grey and splotched with dull orange moss – with hair like wiry pine needles. His nose almost wasn't there at all, from what Torbjorn could see, and a mat of needly forest-green fur stuck out of his shoulders and back. What struck Torbjorn the most were his horrible, smoldering, red-orange eyes, which shined and burned like the inside of his head was a burning brick oven, and Torbjorn, even from so far away, was staring into the flames.

Torbjorn had never seen a troll before – and even now that he was looking at it, he could not believe that the tales he'd heard as a child were real. Trolls turned to stone if they were outside when the sun reached its highest point. Trolls couldn't cross water. Trolls could smell your fear. But above all, a single troll could tear apart an army of men and eat their bones. Suddenly the emerging dawn felt like a bad dream.

The stone finger, he thought, remembering the finger on Rotte's door back in Viksfjord.

The troll struggled at the chains and rasped deep inside its throat. It was the sound of boulder scraping on boulder – an eerie warning to the men who waited on the land in the village. There was only a stone's throw of water separating the village from the beast. Once it got on land…

Then a second horrible rasping came from the furthest ship. On its deck was chained another troll, this one with light-brown skin, just as hideous as the first. There were not one, but two creatures of doom.

A cloaked man came to the bow of the foremost ship, just out of reach of the chained troll. It was Rotte the Righteous. "We come with iron and with thunder, and with beasts that shake the earth beneath!"

It was an intimidation tactic, but the sight of Rotte only made Torbjorn more furious. He wished he'd had a bow; he would shoot an arrow straight into Rotte's eye.

Then, out of the cluster of huts to the north, just where Torbjorn had meant to hide, there charged a tall, fur-clad man heaving a wooden cart in front of him down the slope like a tumbling boulder. The cart was piled high with straw and wood; it smashed into the beach when the wheel hit the sand, and the contents tumbled and spilled onto the ground in one pile. It was Storfjell.

Fool, thought Torbjorn; he was afraid for him. Storfjell was nearly within arrow's reach, and for what?

Then Torbjorn thought he saw in the wreckage of the cart and the pile of straw nine carved and polished handles affixed to nine barrels – the Nine Butter Churns of Asgard.

Storfjell took from his belt a smoldering torch, and thrust it into the straw like a dagger. The flame caught hold like it was starving, flashing red-hot, roaring over the top of the dry straw and devouring it like a pack of wolves tasting reindeer for the first time. The churns went with it, the flame taking hold so fast, the straw burned up and was gone.

Within moments, all that remained were nine black skeletons scattered across each other like bones inside the growing wall of flame.

"Storfjell!" cried Torbjorn. There was no time to put out the crackling fire, even if Torbjorn had dared to race to the water's edge. The enemy was too close; it would be like running under a giant's foot.

And in a moment more, the Nine Churns of Asgard were charred and broken. They burned up into smoldering coals and ash that blew away with the smoke on the breeze.

"Fool!" cried someone hidden up in the rocks.

Then a low moan broke from the south side of the valley. It was a moan of despair and sadness, long and deep, the kind one makes at the loss of a kinsman. It grew louder, and it pierced Torbjorn in the heart like a sad song. It spread across the rocks, curving up to the north and circling the narrow bay, as one Smordaler passed it on to the other, their hearts breaking inside for Smordal's hope and way of life. It grew deeper, as if generations of Smordaler – all the way back from when the Wanderer first gave them the Shining Apple as a gift – joined in the mournful song.

Torbjorn's own brother had done the unthinkable. Storfjell, of all the clan, had been loyal to their ways and filled with the pride of Smordal. And now he had betrayed them all.

Storfjell turned to the waiting ships. "Behold! The Nine Churns of Asgard are destroyed! Smordal holds nothing for you!" he cried.

Torbjorn rushed at Storfjell, not caring how close to the clutches of the Blodkriger he came. He smashed into him with his shoulder from behind, knocking him to the sand.

Storfjell turned and picked himself up, his face and beard covered in flecks of pale yellow sand. There was very little surprise in his grey eyes. Just steady, clear vision.

"Storfjell, what have you done?" gasped Torbjorn.

"That which had to be," said Storfjell.

Torbjorn shook his head. This was not his brother. "But Smordal…. The churns… Storfjell, what have you done?" he said again.

"That which you forced me to do," said Storfjell.

The words cut deep. Rotte's smile at Viksfjord flashed into his mind. Torbjorn knew his brother spoke true. This was the end of the work which Torbjorn had begun when he'd given up their secret.

There was a sudden rush; something charged toward Torbjorn. It was warrior of Smordal, a shrill battle cry in his throat, his spear raised and aimed at Storfjell's heart.

Torbjorn reacted instinctively. He swung his spade at the attacker's legs from the front, catching him at the ankles and tripping him up just enough to make him falter. Storfjell dodged, leaping to one side with his back arched. The attacker's spear lunged into empty air. He fell to the ground.

It was Mannkraft's son, Grimbarn. "Are you for Smordal, or for them?" he shouted.

Storfjell never answered. An arrow whistled through the air and with a loud *thunk!* drove itself into the wooden cart right next to Storfjell's back. Torbjorn turned to face the ships.

"Attack!" came a shrill cry from the ships. It was a cry filled with rage and revenge. All at once, the men brandished their iron swords, their blades pointed skyward so that the ship looked like a fierce falcon with bristling metal feathers. Then the first ship molted its iron plumage, the men pouring over the side, lowering themselves into the water and wading ashore.

Storfjell stood. "We must flee," said Torbjorn. They would be storming up the beach in no time. The ship itself was nearing the edge of the waterline. From what Torbjorn could tell, it was a flat-bottomed raiding vessel. Raiders used boats like those in the south so they could beach themselves and the men could rush the shore to make a quick attack in one devastating wave. What was worse – it meant the troll could come ashore without crossing the water.

The drums of Smordal beat up in the rocks, and a volley of arrows rained down into the wave of Blodkrig warriors on the sand.

Half of the Blodkrig warriors on the sand fell, hit by the hailstorm of arrows. The wave of men slowed, scattered and fell. A new wave surged forward from the ship.

Torbjorn felt a thrill of hope. Perhaps they did stand a chance. Perhaps they could stand against the Blodkriger once again.

Then the volley ceased and there was no more.

Of course, thought Torbjorn, his heart sinking once again. The archers of Smordal had no doubt used up every last arrow in that single burst. The volley had bought them precious seconds, but nothing more.

"To Farstigen!" cried Father from a cluster of boulders near the center of the village. He was there on the front lines, as close to the enemy as any of them. A different, faster drum beat sounded. They were calling the retreat.

"We must go," shouted Storfjell, picking up Grimbarn and putting him on his feet. Grimbarn pushed him away. The second wave of enemies had reached the shore now; there were only seconds.

"Coward," Grimbarn spat, then ran, leaving his spear in the sand.

"Sometimes, Brother, it is better to live than to fight," said Storfjell to Torbjorn. "And others, it is better to fight than to live. Now you may choose." He ran.

Torbjorn did not quite understand his brother. Was he a coward, or a warrior?

Torbjorn grabbed Grimbarn's discarded spear and kicked off the sand, running toward the fields in his brother's footsteps.

The men were in full retreat around them. Running, with shields at their backs and spear points bobbing up and down.

Torbjorn passed the men who had been hiding near the smokehouse. He could hear the enemies' cries in his ears.

"Brother!" said Storfjell, and suddenly Storfjell turned toward the beach and pointed his spear. By instinct, Torbjorn ducked.

He turned and had just enough time to point his spear straight into the broad wooden shield of a charging warrior. The man's sword was drawn, and his iron helmet pulled low so that half his face was hidden. Torbjorn's spear slammed into the wood; the force of the warrior's run knocked Torbjorn backward off his feet.

Torbjorn fell onto his back in the sand. For a moment, he had the sickening feeling that a sword would come down on him, so he leapt to his feet as fast as he could, with nothing but half a shattered spear in his hand. Luckily, the warrior had been knocked over by the collision too; Torbjorn made it to his feet first. Before the man could raise his sword, Torbjorn swung the butt of his spear crossways, smashing the man in the helmet and knocking him flat on the ground.

"Watch out!" cried Torbjorn. A second warrior came from behind and swung his sword at Storfjell. Storfjell blocked with his spear, then punched the man in the face, knocking him over.

"Retreat!" cried Storfjell.

There were more men coming up fast. The second wave of Blodkriger – twice as large as the first – charged up the sand toward them, their iron swords raised like hooks in the air. Behind them more warriors poured out of the ships to replace those who had fallen on the sand.

Torbjorn turned and ran as fast as he could force himself to run. He charged into the clover field and up the rise, scrambling up a low set of rocks onto a higher hill, scraping his hands badly as he went. He had no time to find the best route – there was no time for that. He had to run, charging like a bull over a narrow berm on the hill and then onward through the field.

Storfjell and his clansmen streamed past him on all sides, running for their lives, shields at their backs, spears in hand. He could not see where Father had gone – he hadn't seen him since he called the retreat. Torbjorn hoped he too had made his escape.

He ran harder, as if he were chased by dragons, but felt as if his legs were made of lead. His chest burned. His feet ached. He could almost feel the points of the enemies' swords in his back, and feared that were he to falter even for an instant, it would be the end.

The narrow pass between two cliffs that marked the foot of Farstigen was just ahead. He dared not look behind him again.

He reached the end of the clover, leapt past two men, and scrambled up the rocks between the two short cliffs. The hard, sharp rocks of the narrow pass never felt so good under Torbjorn's cloth-wrapped feet.

There was a scraping of stone and a pounding of thunder behind him. He spun around to see more of his clan squeezing between the rocks. Behind them, boulders were raining down from above, tumbling onto the swiftest five Blodkrig warriors who'd outpaced their clan.

Torbjorn looked up. There were two of the Smordaler – Gradfir's nephews – shoving more boulders off the cliffs onto the attackers below. It worked: the stones fell and found their targets, knocking three enemy warriors over and smashing them into the ground just behind Torbjorn's heels.

Mannkraft stood below the cliffs, spinning his spear at the enemy, slashing and striking with such great fury that it blinded Torbjorn's sight. Two more enemies fell under Mannkraft's might.

Father was ahead, up on the first switchback in the path, waving men onward with his spear, his hay beard tied back behind him. *He escaped*, thought Torbjorn. "Climb!" boomed Father, "To the paths you know! To the cliffs and woods!"

The men of Smordal flocked to him, all as one, their horned helmets and their weapons at their belts jangling as they streamed into the narrow pass from the field, up the paths, and onward, some turning right, others left as the paths split and twisted their way up the cliffs.

Torbjorn followed them, ignoring his tired, heaving chest, and willing himself upward, climbing into the winding maze of Farstigen and away from his home.

Chapter 11 — The Ruin of Smordal

Torbjorn stayed close on Storfjell's heels as they crisscrossed the maze of narrow paths that led up the face of Farstigen. He hugged the cliff face as closely as he could – there was little room for error when the edge of the precipice was crumbling at your feet. Some of the paths led to the top, others to dead ends that broke away into nothing but ruin for those who dared go down them. Still others wound away into far valleys and were lost.

Torbjorn wondered how Mother, Gudrunn, and Eldrid had fared, especially with a herd of bovines following so closely behind them. Luckily the women and children had such a head start, they were certainly well into the forest by now.

They came to yet another fork in the path. This time Storfjell turned right. The paths hadn't been familiar to Torbjorn for the last half of the day. The clan had long since scattered across them. He had not seen the village for more than an hour either, since the cliffs folded back on themselves, and only caught glimpses of men climbing up above and beneath him. The paths had led them into the crags and fissures in the cliff, making it impossible to tell who was below – Blodkrig warriors or men of Smordal.

"Look!" said Storfjell. Torbjorn turned the corner behind his brother. Several of their clan were gathered up ahead on a sharp bend where the path switched back up the mountain. There was room enough to stand there. Father was with them, perched on the rocks above. They were gazing down into the valley, their shields and spears lowered. Mannkraft stood in the middle of the men, his neck bent and his chin on his chest. He was pointing into the valley below.

What Torbjorn saw there nearly broke his heart.

Far below in the valley of Smordal, cradled between the cliffs at the end of the fjord, where the moon had watched over it just the night before, beyond the crisp fields of clover, the only village Torbjorn had ever loved burned and glowed as fires roared across it, engulfing the longhouse, the stables, and the lodges in an orange-red flame and casting a crimson hue on the Blodkrig warriors who had gathered to watch the village burn.

A thick column of rolling black smoke climbed into the air. Smordal was gone. His village. The place where Torbjorn was meant to spend his life. The place where his people had lived for generations. This was not meant to be! Now, they truly had nothing. Torbjorn hung his head.

"You!" said Mannkraft, looking up from the village to Storfjell. His voice bellowed into a roar, and his face grew dark: "You defied the Wanderer. You turned your back on the destiny of Smordal! All that is left for us now is our wives and children and herds! How shall we feed them? Even our village is burning in flames!" Mannkraft drew his spear. "You shall ever be known as the Ruin of Smordal!"

Whatever safety the clan should have offered vanished, and suddenly, Mannkraft was as fierce as an enemy warrior.

"The Blodkriger will not follow," said Storfjell quietly. He looked directly into Mannkraft's eyes. Torbjorn did not know how he stayed so calm in the face of such anger. "They wanted the Nine Churns. Now they are gone. Farstigen has given us an escape. There is nothing for them here. You can see that as well as I do."

From the bend in the path, the entire cliff below came into view. Storfjell was right. There were no men climbing it. The enemy warriors were all in the village below. They had not followed.

"All for what? So we can die in the wilderness? Without food or livelihood?" cried Mannkraft. He pointed his spear at Storfjell's heart. "Be gone from us, Ruin of Smordal."

Torbjorn clenched the half spear handle he still held in his hands. He wanted to lash out at Mannkraft. How could Mannkraft speak such things to his brother? Storfjell had destroyed the churns. Yes, it had been foolish and rash and even cowardly. Yes, Torbjorn felt betrayed, but it was Torbjorn that had brought this upon them to begin with.

Now there were so many things he wanted to shout and say; he was boiling in anger, his heart swimming in a mixture of rage and guilt. Without thinking, he hurled the broken spear handle at Mannkraft. It bounced off Mannkraft's shield and fell on the rocks.

And then Torbjorn understood. Storfjell had given them a way out. He had given them a choice.

Mannkraft's eyes slanted downward. "And you! The one who betrayed our secret to begin with! Be gone both of you! And this clan will seek safety without such thorns in its side!"

Torbjorn looked to Father, who leaned on his spear. Father turned his eyes away. The simple glance sent a shot of pain into Torbjorn's chest. Wasn't he going to defend them? "Now is not the time for judgment," said Father.

"You let your wisdom waver because they are your sons," said Mannkraft.

"No. You let your wrath rule you when our clan is alone in the wilderness!" said Father. "They will face justice when we've found refuge. If it is the clan's will, they will be exiled."

"It is our will now," said Mannkraft. The men behind Mannkraft banged their spears on the rocks.

Father looked over them, his eyes filling with sorrow. "Is it your will?" he asked.

"Yah!" they said, all at once. It was hardly the entire clan, but it was enough.

Father sighed. There was nothing he could do. A chief could not defy his clan. This was a time for action, not healing, and the clan had spoken. Torbjorn looked to his brother for some sign of hope. Storfjell's face was quiet with stern resolve. His cheeks flexed under his silvery beard and his wrinkles fell. "If that is the will of Smordal," said Father.

"It is," said Mannkraft. He turned up the path, taking a fork that climbed to the left. The men followed him, and in moments, they had turned the corner and passed out of sight.

Father looked down to Torbjorn and Storfjell. He put his hand over his heart, left it there for several seconds, and with sad eyes, turned and took the path after the clan he had sworn to lead.

"Father," said Torbjorn. Father did not return. Torbjorn and Storfjell stood on the bend in the path, alone.

"Did not Father always teach us that family blood is thickest?" muttered Torbjorn.

"Sometimes, a man must do not what he wants to do, but what must be done," said Storfjell.

Torbjorn's heart felt heavy. Was that all Storfjell could say? Another one of his wise and important sayings? Torbjorn kicked a stone and it went sailing over the cliff's edge. He was angry at Mannkraft, and he was angry at Father. He was angry at Storfjell for burning the churns, and most of all, he was angry that he'd set in motion Smordal's defeat by giving up their secret.

"I fear that the names Torbjorn and Storfjell will become bad magic for so long as the generations of Smordal live," muttered Torbjorn. "They'll become curses on our clansmen's tongues." If they sang songs about them now, he would not want to hear them.

"So long as they are alive to despise us," said Storfjell. His mustache curved – it was almost the hint of a smile.

There was a glimmer of truth inside what Storfjell said. The Blodkriger had not followed. Farstigen proved too much for them now that there were no churns to chase. Storfjell had been trying to give the Smordaler a way out. There was hope in his act of cowardice.

Torbjorn wondered for half a moment if he should thank his brother. He decided against it. It was too soon, and there were many miles ahead of them before they would know if they or the clan could live.

They chose the right fork in the path – opposite the fork their clan took. It sloped downward gradually, then rose upward steeply, climbing through a jagged gap between rocks. Torbjorn and Storfjell picked their way carefully through the gap, then for several more hours climbed up the cliffs, taking more than a few wrong turns, until eventually they touched the edge of a snowpack where the trail leveled off and passed into a forest. All at once, they were on level ground.

They had climbed Farstigen.

The air was colder up here. Without the sea to bring its muggy warmth, it had thinned and grown crisp. Storfjell put his hands on his knees and puffed, his breath lingering like a faint fog until it faded away.

Torbjorn stared into the forest. The firs were dark and green and grew so that they cast shadows on each other, leaving the snow speckled with a tangled silhouette of trunks and branches.

"I have never seen the top of Farstigen before. I am glad to know it has an end," puffed Torbjorn.

"Nor have I," said Storfjell. "I cannot say what danger this forest holds."

Torbjorn's cloth-wrapped feet crunched through the thin layer of snow as they entered the trees. The firs were spaced far enough apart that they could pick a path through them without tangling their cloaks, but the shadows dimmed Torbjorn's sight.

It wasn't long before they found a wide, hard-packed track beaten into the snow. "The herd must have been here," said Storfjell, "and maybe Father too. They are ahead of us."

There were rows of hoof prints and footprints scattered along the hard-packed snow. It was clear that several dozen people had come this way not long before. It would have been next to impossible for such a large group to hide their tracks.

Torbjorn and Storfjell followed the path. It carved a steady route through the trees until it turned sharply to the right at the base of a steep granite cliff. They scrambled up some low boulders to a place where the path narrowed. The clan surely had gone single file here, one bovine at a time. The snow set more heavily on the boulders; in some places it had piled up high enough to form thick layers. Whoever had led the clan must have plowed through the waist-high snow one step at a time. It would have been arduous work.

"It looks like a delicious creamy topping that I would like to put on some of Mother's floppy pancakes," said Torbjorn, pointing to the snow-covered boulders.

"If only we could eat rocks, then our bellies would ever be full," replied Storfjell.

Torbjorn laughed. "You make me hungry," he said. He'd realized he hadn't eaten since the night before, when they'd drunk the fresh Nectar of Moo around the campfire. No wonder he his belly felt too hot, and his head felt sluggish. They had travelled so far. "I have some bread," he said. He had brought a little with him.

"Then let us eat it and rest," said Storfjell, "but only for a moment." They plunked down on a boulder in the snow, their backs turned to the clan's path and their eyes on the forest path below them. Torbjorn unwrapped the bundle he had wound in a cloth and tied under his cloak. The loaf was half-eaten, and cold, but it would cover their hunger for a little while at least. Best of all, Torbjorn had slit it down the middle lengthwise and smeared it between the two halves with the golden butter of Smordal.

He broke off a piece and gave it to Storfjell. When Storfjell opened it, he began to cry.

His tears were soft and faint at first. Then they grew, and Storfjell bent his head; his chest chugged up and down as he sobbed. His tears fell heavily into the snow, melting their way into the cold powder and leaving behind tiny vertical burrows, like an ant tunneling underground, before they disappeared.

Torbjorn did not understand. "This is it," said Storfjell. "The last time we will taste the Golden Fortune of our Herds."

Torbjorn felt his eyes push tears outward, though he would not let them go. A great sadness grabbed hold of his heart, and he felt as if this were somehow the end of things. His clan would have little to trade at Viksfjord anymore. Without the butter, their blueberry muffins could not have the power or taste to command the price they had before. It would take two, or three, or ten baskets of muffins to get the same price they'd gotten from just one basket before. That meant ten times the crop they'd have to glean from the field, and ten times the manpower. It would be impossible to make anywhere near that many muffins in a season. They would have nothing to trade. They would have no way to get clothes, tools or meat that they did not make or raise themselves. They would starve.

For a moment, anger kindled in Torbjorn's heart against his brother. But then, Storfjell sobbed again, and Torbjorn knew that worst of all those things was that Storfjell must have known how bad it would be. He must have known what he was doing to the clan when he'd burned the churns. His sobs were all the proof that Torbjorn needed of Storfjell's sorrow.

"You did what you must, Brother," said Torbjorn. He meant what he said. Storfjell had given them a way out. Had they stayed in the village, they would have been slaughtered. Now that they were far away, tasting the last of the butter, Storfjell's tears crashing to the snow, Torbjorn knew that it was true. He knew that there had been no other way.

"Or I have traded a quick death for a slow and painful one," sobbed Storfjell.

"There will be ways!" said Torbjorn. He did not know how, but their clan would learn to survive again. They would find a new livelihood. Yes, they were without churns or lands now, and their homes had all been burned, but Torbjorn vowed in his heart to find a way for his people to survive. They must.

Storfjell put his head on his knees. His bread was untouched.

Just then there was a faint moan from far away. Torbjorn turned toward the sound. It was a high sound, long and loud, like something was in pain. Then there was another moan much like it at the same time, but deeper and shorter. Torbjorn recognized it now.

"Bovines!" said Storfjell. He stood up, shook off his tears, and strode toward the moans. Torbjorn packed up what few morsels of bread remained and followed. He knew the sounds of their herd. Those were the moos of bovines in peril.

Storfjell left the packed path and plowed through the waist-deep snow in the direction of the moans. The snow was thick, like wading through mounds of cold, dry beans, and the going looked hard for Storfjell. They came up and over a small rise that blocked their view of the forest until they got to the other side.

They slid down the far side of the embankment, plowing huge cakes of snow with them as they went. At the bottom, they stopped to listen. The snow absorbed most of the sound, leaving the forest eerie and quiet. Then more moans from the east. They were louder. Torbjorn and Storfjell were getting close.

The two brothers turned and followed alongside a slight depression in the snow. Torbjorn had to lift his knee up straight out of the snow to pull his foot free with each step, so it was slow going. Something about the snow underneath was softer here; it made it feel like the ground was lying to him.

They slogged forward until they got to a set of pines growing tightly together. Torbjorn could hear the gurgling of water somewhere in the forest, though he couldn't see any streams. The moaning grew more desperate. Now he was certain the bovines were in trouble; he urged Storfjell to hurry.

Past the pines, the ground fell away steeply. The snow had collapsed there, so that a ledge of snow was left overhanging a bare

dirt cliff face about as high as Storfjell's head. Roots grew out of the
dirt and curled into the crisp thin air. At the foot of the dropoff was a
stream that ran from underneath the deep banks of snow.

Torbjorn stood carefully behind his brother – he did not want
the ground to collapse beneath him – and leaned out ever so slightly
to get a better look. Down below, standing knee-deep in a cold
mountain stream, were two bovines, shivering and wet, with steam
rising off their backs.

They were milk-bovines: one a spotted brown, the other reddish.
The reddish one was the very same Torbjorn had kissed on the
forehead when he'd left the herd back in the valley of Smordal.

"The spotted one I believe is called Smakkerdette," said
Torbjorn. "And the red one is Melkhjert."

Smakkerdette mooed pitifully; Torbjorn almost began to cry like
Storfjell had. He swallowed his feelings; he was a warrior now, and
there was no place in a warrior's path for weakness, only action.

Without waiting for Storfjell, Torbjorn leapt down the
embankment, skidding along the dirt to slow his fall. He managed to
hit a spot of soggy ground next to the stream, where his feet sunk
into the mud. The reddish milk-bovine looked at him sadly, her
nostrils flaring.

Torbjorn had spent enough time with the herd to sense a
bovine's mood. "Poor, sad bovine," he said, and patted her head
softly. He stroked her ears, and she nuzzled her muzzle into his side.

The spotted brown bovine was pawing at the earth on the other
side of the bank. The snow had collapsed there too, and there were
big sheets of ice floating, up-ended, in the stream. "The snow here
betrayed them, and they fell," said Storfjell. The bovines must have
strayed from the herd and been trapped there.

Torbjorn reached out to the spotted brown bovine. She was a strong, beautiful beast, with toned shoulders and haunches that flexed every time she pawed the stream, and dark eyelashes that were long and curled upward, like she'd been decorated for the village festivals Torbjorn had seen in Viksfjord.

"Here, push her up the bank, and we will set them both aright on their eight hooves again!" said Storfjell.

He wrapped his arms around the spotted brown Smakkerdette, set his feet as well as he could in the mud, then lifted. She was not like lifting a butterfly, but Torbjorn was a Smordaler, fed on the Nectar of Moo which came from the bovines who grazed in the crisp green clover of Smordal. Years of nourishment gave his incredible eight-foot frame great strength.

Smakkerdette's hooves came out of the water. She was probably six boulders in weight. Torbjorn had lifted sheep before, and goats he could toss over the pond into the pasture to save himself the trip, but a bovine itself he had never hefted. She was heavy.

She mooed and then stuck out her tongue, but did not protest more.

He pulled Smakkerdette over to his side of the stream, and, bending at the knees, hunched himself lower so he could lift her from below her belly. He heaved her up above his shoulders to the ledge above him, and strained to hold her in place.

"Pull," he said through gritted teeth. Storfjell hugged Smakkerdette around the middle, then hoisted her up the rest of the way and set her onto flat, snowy ground. She sank up to her shoulders.

Torbjorn leaned back against the dirt to catch his breath. His arms were throbbing with the exertion, and his neck was tight as a wound chord from clenching his jaw.

"Well done, Brother!" said Storfjell. "Now again!"

Torbjorn puffed. He was not sure he could. Storfjell should be the one below; he was the largest brother. Nevertheless, Torbjorn patted Melkhjert on the head, and whispered in her ear. "This is to save you, my glorious bovine," he said.

She smelled his hand, then bit him gently.

"By the world!" cried Torbjorn. The bite did not hurt, but it was unexpected. He never thought of himself as being a succulent leaf of clover.

"This Melkhjert likes you!" said Storfjell.

"Hmph," muttered Torbjorn. *What a fine way to show it.* He considered biting her back. Instead, he bent his knees and caught her around the ribs and lifted, just as he'd done before.

Melkhjert was even heavier than Smakkerdette. But Torbjorn had a better plan this time, and he leaned up against the ledge for support. It worked, and he was able to pass Melkhjert to Storfjell with only half as much trouble as before. She let out a long, breathy moo. Torbjorn felt a little like he was squeezing moos out of a goatskin flask. He almost laughed at the thought, but he could not spare the breath.

"Now, help me, Brother," said Torbjorn. He reached his hand up and Storfjell grabbed his wrist. Storfjell pulled. Torbjorn kicked up the dirt, and scrambling, landed fairly easily with his top half in the snow on the ledge.

Melkhjert clamped the hem of his cloak in her mouth and pulled, as if to help Torbjorn up. He stood. "She is clever," said Torbjorn.

"Perhaps the cleverest of all the herd, if you ask Mooverk," said Storfjell.

"At least all of the clan does not banish us," smiled Torbjorn.

"Yes, now we have friends," said Storfjell. His eyes turned up at the corners. He was smiling inside.

Smakkerdette turned and mooed at them, nuzzling Storfjell's woolen pants. "And of course we will not forget you," said Torbjorn. It was somehow comforting, to have members of the herd with them. It felt in a little way like a piece of home. Two outcast brothers with two bovines that had strayed from the herd.

Storfjell led the two bovines back toward the path. The brothers kept Melkhjert and Smakkerdette behind them in single file while Storfjell broke through the snow. It was slow going. Smakkerdette's legs sunk down like posts in the ground more than once, and she nearly landed on her chin twice. It made Torbjorn wonder how anything four-footed ever walked at all.

When they got back to the main path they rested. Torbjorn could hear the din of camp being set for the night above them on top of the granite cliff.

"Storfjell, it is our clan!" said Torbjorn.

"Aye," said Storfjell.

There were commands coming from a strong voice – probably Mannkraft's – and the stamping and mooing of cattle, and the felling of lumber. It was hard to hide an entire village of men, women and children as it moved through the forest, even with the snow buffering the sound.

"Perhaps we should take these bovines to them," said Torbjorn.

Storfjell shook his head. "No. Not unless we were to do it in secret. The clan has spoken against us, and we would not kindle their wrath further."

"Then we can make camp here tonight as well, at the base of this cliff," said Torbjorn. He wondered if he'd ever see his family again.

"Yes, we will rise early and leave the bovines with the herd before our clan wakes."

They used their knives to cut fresh boughs from the fir trees to lay on the cold snow. The boughs would help keep them dry as they huddled through the cold night.

And night was coming. The sun had already begun to dip toward the horizon and cast that grey spell of twilight. The trees and shadows mingled together as the colors faded. In a few hours, the sun would be gone, and night would swallow the forest.

The bovines stood nearby as they worked. It reminded Torbjorn of all the times they'd worked together in the fields.

All at once, Melkhjert's tail stiffened and she turned on her hoof. She stared into a copse of trees in the forest downhill from where they stood. The mountain was divided there. A protruding vein of granite, no more than twice Torbjorn's height jutted out of the ground all the way from the copse to the wide cliff where Storfjell and Torbjorn had made camp. Melkhjert mooed. This time it was a soft high-pitched moo that sounded like a warning.

"I do not speak the Bovine like Mooverk," said Storfjell, "but I fear our hoofed companion is warning us."

Smakkerdette stamped her feet like she was agitated about something as well. Just then, the boulders moved. It was difficult to tell in the grey light, but Torbjorn was almost certain that the trees moved with them. He rubbed his eyes and squinted. "What magic…?" he said.

Then the boulders moved again along the granite vein. He was certain this time. "Storfjell, there is something there."

Storfjell nodded, raising his spear and pulling a small axe from his belt. Torbjorn unsheathed his knife.

They stepped back until they were hidden against the tree trunks, and shushed the bovines. Melkhjert and Smakkerdette got quiet. Something was amiss.

The rocks stopped moving, and the trees with them, and all went deadly silent. Then, two sets of glowing, burning-red coal eyes suddenly opened in the darkness. It was like staring into a furnace of melting heat and brimstone. It was the eyes of the trolls.

Chapter 12 — The Trolls

Torbjorn flattened himself up against the tree so hard, he nearly pressed himself into the bark. All hope he'd had that they'd outrun the danger snapped and shattered into fear. Warriors were one thing. He and Storfjell maybe could even fight half a dozen of them at a time. But these were trolls, and to face a troll was death.

"They must've climbed up the cliffs," whispered Storfjell. "The men could not, but these creatures are born of rock and earth. Such is their kinship with it, that they have no fear of the precipice."

"What will we do?" asked Torbjorn. It was a moment when he realized that he needed his brother, and for once, he was glad that he was not the oldest.

Storfjell held up his hand for silence. The two trolls scraped across the rocks like boulders tumbling slowly up the hill; in the waning light, it seemed that the granite itself was moving. Torbjorn might have believed his eyes were fooling him, had not the trolls opened their own burning eyes, which glowed in the twilight and spoke of red-hot Muspelheim, the Fire Realm itself.

The rocks led to the wide cliff, a direct and clear path to the camp above their heads.

"Our clan. Do the trolls know they are there?" whispered Torbjorn.

"I think not yet," said Storfjell. "They wander, tasting the rock for signs, but they do not know how close they have come."

Torbjorn thought of Father, Mother, and his sisters above. They would be caught by surprise. Mannkraft would surely fight the troll and be slain. "We cannot let them get to the camp, Brother," said Torbjorn. "We must fight them first."

"Torbjorn, you and I, great men of Smordal could not defeat even one troll. To battle a pair of them is folly," said Storfjell.

Torbjorn felt fear grow up his back and choke his neck. *Courage, like your fathers have*, he thought. "Then we will lead them away. If they taste rock and stone, then we will give them our scent to follow through the forests, and we will lead them to forgotten paths."

Storfjell looked Torbjorn in the eyes with his silvery bushy eyebrows furrowed and clenched. "Should we go down that path, we may not return," Storfjell said.

If we do not, thought Torbjorn, *they will sing songs of our deed*. But they would return. They had to.

Storfjell's face went soft. He hooked his axe on his belt, and threw down his spear. He tightened his cloak, bent low, and with a huff heaved Smakkerdette over his shoulders like a sack of grain, her front legs dangling over his right shoulder and her hind legs over his left. He held tightly to her ankles.

It looked almost comical to Torbjorn, to see a bovine on his brother like that, with her udder dangling on his chest like a bouncy sack.

"We cannot leave these behind, or the trolls will slay them," said Storfjell.

Torbjorn nodded. He too crouched down and heaved Melkhjert over his shoulders the same way. She was heavy, and pressed him into the snow. It would make walking hard, but he would have to manage.

Storfjell picked up a rock as big as his fist, and curled his arm back. "Get ready," he said. He heaved the rock up in a long arc toward the trolls.

Torbjorn watched it curve downward then smash into the stone right between the two monsters.

Both troll heads snapped around and looked straight at Torbjorn and Storfjell with glowing red brimstone eyes that seemed to pour fire out of them. The trolls' mouths peeled back and opened, hissing and rasping with a loud, threatening growl that echoed through the forest.

"Fiends of stone!" cried Storfjell. He turned to Torbjorn. "Run!" he said.

Torbjorn had already started. He pushed off the snow, and darted to the southeast, somewhere between the beaten path and the depression in the stream where they'd saved the bovines. He wanted to make sure they stayed far enough off the path that led to the clan. They would have to run through the fresh snow.

He plowed through the drifts, pushing aside barrelfuls of snow with his thighs at each step. Melkhjert bobbed up and down on his back, her ribs and hips jamming into his shoulders as he ran. *Not fast enough*, thought Torbjorn. He could feel Storfjell right behind him. And behind his brother? The trolls were certain to be there, with grasping claws and chomping jaws. He charged harder still through the snow into an opening between the trees.

The forest was filled with deep, guttural growls and the sound of splintering wood behind them. There was no doubt – the trolls were giving chase. Torbjorn chanced a look back.

A stone's throw behind his brother the fir trees quaked, shivering from their trunks up their branches and into their needles, until with one great *crack* the foremost tree splintered to pieces and fell as the trolls smashed it aside.

And there they roared.

For the first time, in the waning twilight, Torbjorn could see under the open sky just how monstrous they really were. The troll in front was a dark grey rock color. Matted, deep green pine needles stuck out of his rocky back – the perfect camouflage in the forest. The one behind was slightly smaller – though still enormous – his rock-skin light brown and dotted with tiny flecks of muted red.

"Run!" cried Torbjorn, doubling his pace.

He turned and plowed forward in the snow, away from the trolls and deeper into the forest. The needles on the trees clawed at his face and tangled in his beard as he charged onward. His back began to feel hot, and his skin roasted under his furs so that he could not wait for the sweat to come.

He and Storfjell ran on, minute after minute, Torbjorn trying to breathe at a steady pace, trying to resist the urge to stop and walk. Torbjorn chanced another glance back while he ran – this time, he could not see them, though he could still hear their roars in the distance behind them.

He whipped past the trees, and out into another clearing. For the moment, there were no trolls in sight. Torbjorn was beginning to feel tired; he could feel himself getting slower.

His next step broke through the packed layer and went deep into the airy snow beneath. He lost his balance, tipping sideways and nearly dropping Melkhjert.

Melkhjert mooed softly. It was a tender moo, almost like she was urging him onward.

"I'll lead. Come, Brother," said Storfjell, and passed him by, breaking into the snow and forging a path ahead of him.

Torbjorn welcomed the rest. It was much easier to follow his brother's path.

They came out of the trees to a rocky ridge where they could see the last rays of the sun bending over distant mountains. The light glowed orange on the skyline for a moment, then was gone.

"Night," said Storfjell.

As darkness fell they ran onward, the bovines bouncing up and down on their backs. For a few hopeful minutes, Torbjorn did not hear the roar of trolls at their backs. He even began to wonder if they'd lost them. He set down Melkhjert on a boulder overlooking a deep, clear stream, knowing that it could only be for a moment.

"I think we are almost faster than trolls," said Storfjell. He too unloaded his bovine-burden.

"Yes," panted Torbjorn. He and his brother seemed to have gained a lead over the beasts. "They must not be so fast on snow as they are on the rocks. Maybe we have gotten away."

They rested there, not willing or able to force themselves to go on just yet. The stars blinked into view and shined on the snow. It must have been well past midnight. Torbjorn even closed his eyes for a moment, thinking he might sleep, when suddenly, at the edge of a row of jagged boulders, the giant grey troll tore out of the woods and leapt onto the rocks not a boat's length behind them. It snarled.

"This way!" shouted Storfjell. He heaved Smakkerdette up onto his back, turned and skipped down the boulders to the edge of the stream below. Torbjorn was on his feet in a flash, pulling Melkhjert onto his shoulders.

Storfjell plunged into the tumbling water up to his waist. He pushed ahead, wading through up to his chest, the water swirling and beating around him, Smakkerdette raising her head to keep dry. It was madness to plunge into icy water at night. Torbjorn could guess why his brother did it: the lore says trolls can't cross water. They would find out soon enough if that were true.

Torbjorn forced himself to jump into the cold stream. In an instant his chest froze, his lungs tightened, his breath turned to an icicle in his throat and choked him, his mind blanked. His limbs numbed until they were lead. He could not feel Melkhjert on his back. Surely the giant grey troll could smash him from the shore. He forced himself forward. He had to get to dry ground.

He pushed the several remaining arm lengths to the opposite shore. Storfjell reached out his arm and pulled Torbjorn up into the snow.

The grey troll was perched on all fours on the bank they'd just left, hissing and growling at the water's edge.

"So it is true. The water dissuades them," smiled Storfjell.

"Yah!" gasped Torbjorn, trying to catch his breath again. That seemed to be true, and it had saved them, but whatever lead Storfjell and Torbjorn had, it was gone. The trolls had caught up.

"I wonder if as the sun disappears, they run faster," said Storfjell, looking up at the night sky.

It made sense. The legends said that the sun turned trolls to stone. That could not be entirely true, since the sun had shone on the trolls all that day, and the trolls were yet alive and running. Still, there must have been a glimmer of truth in such ancient tales. The lower the sun dipped, the faster the trolls seemed to go. How else had they suddenly run so fast if it weren't for the darkness?

The red troll leapt up and down the rocks on the opposite bank. He scrambled back and forth at the water line, his blunt nose to the ground, his molten eyes darting back and forth, from rock to stream, and worst of all, to Torbjorn. The beast moved twice as quickly as he had in the twilight.

"He's looking for a way to cross," said Storfjell.

"I do not want to be here when he finds it," replied Torbjorn. He stood, hoisted Melkhjert onto his sopping wet back, and ran downstream.

The brothers and the bovines ran into the night for hours, ever leading the trolls southeast and away from their clan. They ran through a wide meadow where the moon shone bright and clear on the snow. They ran through a thicket and back up the next mountain, where they could see the burning eyes of the trolls speeding along in the meadow far below.

Torbjorn was glad they hadn't met the trolls in winter. Only a few months from now, the sun would disappear completely until spring. He dared not think how fast the trolls would be in the dead of a winter's night. "If only we'd met them when the sun was up all night," said Torbjorn.

"But they are here now, and we must run yet in the darkness," said Storfjell. However much Torbjorn didn't like it, Storfjell was right.

The snows in the forest were deeper than they were in the meadow, and Torbjorn once again found himself plowing through drifts. It was hard work, Melkhjert's head bouncing up and down with each of Torbjorn's steps. "You ever think that maybe this might be easier without bovines atop our backs?" asked Torbjorn.

Melkhjert mooed reproachfully. Perhaps it was coincidence, but she seemed to understand what Torbjorn was getting at.

They stopped to take off their loads of bovine and rest from time to time. Crossing the stream had given the brothers a considerable lead. They had not seen the trolls for more than an hour, but they could hear them just beyond the trees, crashing through the forest and groaning as they went.

It seemed that no matter how far they ran, they could not escape the trolls. Torbjorn's bones were beginning to tire. He did not know how much longer he could go.

Chapter 13 — The Brink

They did not stop running until the whole night had passed, and the moon began to fade and the black sky began to soften before the morning light. Their bones were sore and their backs weary. Torbjorn had to focus on lifting his foot with each step, and at times, he found himself lapsing into sleep as he ran, until the whole day and night seemed like one exhausting dream.

Sometime during the night, Torbjorn thought he glimpsed the trolls on a ledge behind them. Torbjorn did not see them until the trolls heaved a boulder the size of sheep at Storfjell's head. It missed, and smashed into a tree next to them, splitting the trunk in two.

All the while as they ran, Torbjorn wondered what the clan would think when they heard of the brave feat he and his brother had done for them. That single thought sustained him. His feet hurt, and the cloth bound around them was beginning to wear thin and tear. He did not want to say it, but he didn't think he could go on much longer.

"Brother," said Torbjorn, "Do you think that the clan will sing songs of our deeds?"

"I do not know that the Clan of Smordal will ever know that we gave our lives for them," said Storfjell.

Torbjorn did not expect Storfjell to say that. *Give our lives*? Is that what Storfjell expected? Torbjorn still hoped they'd find a way out of this. He'd always believed they could. Is that how Storfjell thought it might end? "Then Smordal will never even know what doom we spared them from!" Torbjorn said.

Storfjell was silent, except for his heavy breath and his steps in the snow. Then he spoke. "Do you love our clan because you want them to give you glory, or because you want them to live?" It did not sound like a reproof; it was an honest question.

Torbjorn did not know how to answer. Ever since Storfjell burned the churns, Storfjell had done things for his own mysterious reasons. Storfjell hadn't cared if Mannkraft, or Father, or even the entire clan was against him. He'd only cared about one thing: the life of the clan.

"I..." was all Torbjorn could reply. For many miles and many hours afterward he tried to think of what to say as he trudged over hills, through clearings, and back into the deep forest. He did not know why he was doing this – why he was risking his life on a quest that no one might ever know about, for a clan that had forced him into exile.

They stopped to rest in the forest again in a thicket of trees. Melkhjert's udder had swollen so large, it looked like she was about to lay a giant pink egg. Torbjorn hadn't thought of it until now, but the two bovines had probably not been milked since before they'd left the village. That was a full day and a half ago. It wasn't good to leave a bovine un-milked for long. No doubt the constant bouncing was taking its toll.

Torbjorn would have milked her right then, had not the tops of the trees somewhere behind them shook; a flock of ravens squawked and flew from their roosts. The trolls were near.

So Torbjorn and Storfjell ran on, as weary as they were, until the sun had climbed high above them. Finally, when the color in the forest and sky glowed green and blue, they stopped again to lift the bovines off their backs and rest.

"Now that it is the middle of the day, we can outrun these fiends of stone," said Torbjorn. His feet were bleeding on the snow. He could not run forever.

Storfjell grunted. "We cannot. There must be a clear track for them to follow."

"Why? The sun is at its highest! We can escape them if we hurry," said Torbjorn.

Storfjell shook his head. "But then who knows if they will return and find our clan. We are too close still."

It made sense. They had come far, but the natural way for the trolls to return would be the way they'd come – if they were smart enough to smell the rocks back to their ships. They could easily happen upon the Smordaler again and catch them by surprise.

Torbjorn staggered to his feet. His belly had collapsed inside him. Their last morsels of bread had been ruined while fording the stream. He hadn't eaten anything in so long, his head was beginning to give him strange thoughts and his eyes could not focus for lack of food.

They stumbled on for most of the afternoon, hoping that the sun would keep the trolls at bay as it crawled through the sky. Melkhjert's and Smakkerdette's udders began to look like pink swollen peaches just ripe for the picking. Torbjorn felt sorry for them, even though they did not complain. They crossed meadows, valleys, and mountains, until finally, as the sun was beginning to disappear behind the mountains again, they came to a ridge where the mountain fell steeply away to the east in a wide bowl that curled out on either side.

"Night…" said Storfjell. The word sent shivers through Torbjorn's spine. The trolls would be getting faster. He was so tired.

There was a roar and a crash in the forest behind them. This time, it was closer than before.

"We must use the land to our advantage," said Storfjell. Without more warning than that, he leapt off the edge of the mountain and landed on his back, sliding down the steep mountainside through the snow. Smakkerdette's udder bobbed and jostled up and down as they both slid down the hill, tumbling faster than Torbjorn could ever run.

Torbjorn looked back. There was no mistake about it this time: the trolls were gaining on them. He looked over the edge – it was a very long way to the bottom. Storfjell's slide turned into a tumble; he lost his hold on Smakkerdette. He and she both began to roll, bounce, and jumble down the hill at incredible speeds in two different directions.

The trolls broke out of the forest. The red one rushed in at Torbjorn's left; the grey flanked him on the right. They were trying to cut him off. Torbjorn peered down at his brother below, still sliding and tumbling, and wondered for a moment what it must be like to be bitten by a troll. "You'll not taste me!" he cried, and jumped, feet pointed like an arrow down the mountain.

His back hit first, knocking the wind from his chest. His helmeted head bumped back against Melkhjert's soft ribs, and she cried out in pain. He held as tight as he could to her ankles and tried to keep a straight course. He dug his heels into the snow, hoping to slow himself down. That only sprayed snow up in his face, stinging his eyes so that he had to close them.

The mountain behind him turned downward steeply, and he felt himself go airborne, his stomach lurching upward into his chest, Melkhjert floating above him like an iron cloud. Torbjorn had lost all control. His momentum carried his legs and feet upward, and for a moment, he wondered exactly which way was up.

Then the ground swung up and smashed him on the side. He hit first. Melkhjert landed next – right on top of Torbjorn's gut. She flopped over him, mooing as she landed, two of her legs sprawled out in a way that did not look possible for a bovine. She was wrenched free from his grip.

She flew, tumbling like a boulder in an avalanche down the hill. Torbjorn hit another bump, and went airborne again. He twisted around on his stomach and clawed at the snow, digging in with his fingers to slow his fall. It only half worked, and he kept sliding further and further down the slope.

He hit a rock, bounced upward, dug his heels in, then as the slope gradually leveled out, slowed to a stop.

Torbjorn did not feel well. His wool pants were twisted and pulled up to his armpits. His belt had come unlatched and was lying in the snow next to him. His cloak was tied up in knots around his arms, and his horned helmet had fallen off and was gone. He looked back up at the slope. His helmet was up the mountainside, too far up to retrieve without an hour's worth of climbing. Melkhjert was somewhere in the thicket of trees, mooing in short bursts that sounded almost like crying.

Torbjorn sat up with a groan. His side hurt where Melkhjert had struck him in the gut. He put his hands first on his sides, then his face, then his thighs and knees. He was bruised, battered, beaten, bumbled, but alive. He looked around. His head still turned – that was fortunate.

Storfjell and Smakkerdette were nowhere to be found.

Torbjorn carefully propped himself up on his knees, then stood. He was shaky at first, but his legs seemed to work fine. Then he lifted his arms – those worked too.

"Yah well!" he cried back up at the mountain. That was probably the fastest he'd travelled in his entire life, and the trolls were so far up there, he could not even see them. It was thrilling, to have come so far so fast.

"Mooo-oooo-ooo," cried Melkhjert in short bursts, from somewhere in the trees. It sounded like sobbing.

Torbjorn ran shakily over in the direction of the sound. She was lying on her back behind an old gnarled pine. She looked up at him, her eyes round and wide, her head bobbling around on top of her neck. Her muzzle was turned up at the corners almost in what looked like a smile.

Torbjorn took a step back and cocked his head to one side. Now that he saw her, Melkhjert's crying sounded more like laughter.

"I might even guess that Melkhjert would like to tumble down the mountain again," said Torbjorn.

She mooed a happy moo. It sounded like a yes.

"Do not say that to me, four-footed beast! I am not climbing back up there!" Torbjorn said, pointing to the mountain ledge far above. She chewed, her muzzle going up and down and in a way that looked to Torbjorn almost like she was thinking about what he said.

"Brother, we have not finished yet," said Storfjell from behind Torbjorn. He'd come out of the trees, Smakkerdette in his arms. She had the same giddy look on her face that Melkhjert did. "See!"

Storfjell turned his head and looked up at a rocky ledge that grew vertically out of the top half of the face of the mountain.

Near the top of that ledge, there were what looked like two sets of boulders scraping and falling in short bursts down the rock. "The trolls!" said Torbjorn.

"Yes, they will be quick on the rock, but not so fast as us when they hit the snow, I think," said Storfjell.

"Yah!" grinned Torbjorn, "We were quite fast." His whole body felt like he was glowing with the magic courage of battle, so quick was the slide. "Then let us run."

Melkhjert mooed painfully at him. Her udder was full, fuller than he had ever seen it. It was bulging and the skin was so tight and pink, Torbjorn could almost see right through it. The constant up and down of running in the snow must have agitated it horribly. Even more so, to tumble down a mountainside, it was too much for a bovine to bear.

Smakkerdette looked even worse. She stood in the snow, her blue eyes big and sad. "The pride of Smordal – our herds," said Storfjell, "and they have come to this." He patted her on the head.

"Brother, let us milk our tiny herd of two, and squeeze their udders so they do not suffer such milk-pains," said Torbjorn.

"And then perhaps we can drink a little for some nourishment, for today we will need our strength," nodded Storfjell. His lower lids had sunk into shadow beneath his eyes. His cheeks had lost the orange hue they usually had. Storfjell looked as tired as Torbjorn felt.

Storfjell took a step forward. Then, without warning, he collapsed onto his knees and fell face-first like a tree into the snow.

Torbjorn rushed to him and knelt by his side. "Brother! Speak to me!" he said. He pushed his hands like spades under Storfjell and pried him over, rolling him onto his back.

Storfjell's eyes were closed. His lips trembling out faint traces of frosty air. He was alive, but as worn as shoe leather that's walked too many miles on stony earth.

Torbjorn pressed the palms of his hands onto Storfjell's cheeks. He did not stir. "Brother!" cried Torbjorn. *Was he dead?* There was still breath in him, but he did not wake.

The trolls were coming. Torbjorn could not carry two bovines and his brother too. He barely had strength to walk himself. He was stranded, it would be night soon, and suddenly, he felt all alone.

Torbjorn straightened his brother's arms and laid his cloak underneath Storfjell's neck. He didn't know what else to do. He felt stupid and helpless. He never should have started this chase. Now his brother was lying there in the snow, maybe even dead from exhaustion.

Torbjorn slumped down on a patch of bare ground and hung his head. He would have to wait for him to wake.

Melkhjert pressed her muzzle into Storfjell's cheek. She looked so sad in the growing darkness.

Torbjorn smoothed out Melkhjert's reddish fur. It had become matted and tangled during the past few days. She did not deserve this. *Poor, poor Melkhjert*, thought Torbjorn, and in despair, he did the only thing he could think to do – he would milk her. It was the least he could do for such a loyal bovine.

He led her onto flat ground where he stamped out a patch of firm snow. He knelt on one knee, and like he had learned when he was very young, grasped two of the four teats hanging from her udder. Mooverk had often talked of how gentle one must be when milking the bovines, and Torbjorn tried to remember all of his words.

He squeezed from the base of the teat downward. It felt firmer than he would have expected, and it took more force to push the milk out than he remembered. A dribble of watery, yellow milk leaked out the hole in the bottom of the rightmost teat.

Then, Melkhjert mooed a long and sad moo, like she was speaking for all the bovines of the herd, and saying the thing they had kept inside their hearts for centuries. Torbjorn squeezed again; She mooed again, and this time, out came a thick, yellow cream that dripped in soft, oversized pearls, like golden dewdrops onto the crisp white snow. It shined in the moonlight.

What have I done? wondered Torbjorn. He had never seen anything like this come from an udder. Perhaps he had milked her wrong. Perhaps Melkhjert was hurt. Perhaps his weariness had so far overcome him now, he was not seeing things as they really were. He might have believed that too, if the golden drops were not so beautiful and somehow… familiar.

"Brother," whispered Torbjorn. If only Storfjell were awake.

Torbjorn squeezed out another golden, creamy stream into his hand, and it piled up there like a smooth mountain of thick honey. He put it to his cracked and bleeding lips.

When it touched them it was like a warmth he had never known. While it was on his tongue all the sorrows and terror of the battle and the defeat of his people melted away, and he felt like a child again. It tasted creamy and sweet like honey, but salty like the sea. If snow could be warm, this was it. It was more than a taste – it was an embrace.

Something he had tasted before was hidden inside the golden creamy drops. Something he had known and loved, magnified into its full potential. Then he realized it: butter.

What Melkhjert had given him was not just milk; somehow it was butter.

Somewhere deep in her heart she had found a way to bless her masters with more than milk. And what was inside the swollen pink udder that hung from her belly was a glowing gift of life. A sun on the horizon.

Never had the Nine Churns of Asgard given life to the Nectar of Moo like the golden dewdrops that melted on his tongue right now.

Torbjorn swallowed, and his throat felt warm, then his belly. He could feel strength spreading outward, from his stomach to his limbs and out his bones. It glowed. Then, like a coal in the winter, it faded away.

He needed more. He squeezed Melkhjert's udder again, and a fresh stream of thick golden butter squirted into his open palm. He squeezed, and squeezed, milking her until he had a glob of butter curled up in his hand.

Then he ate, scooping up the smooth butter with his tongue and half chewing, half drinking it. The butter covered the insides of his mouth in a smooth, rich film. His belly felt warm strength again. It grew out across his body, stronger this time, until it reached his fingertips – a rejuvenating sensation, as if it were sleep washing out through his blood. The soreness and knots in his back and shoulders slowly unraveled, smoothed, and faded away. He ate.

Melkhjert mooed a happy moo, and Torbjorn lay on the ground beneath her udder, milking her so that the creamy butter squirted straight into his open mouth. He closed his eyes and drank as quickly as he could, until finally, what seemed like hours later, his hunger was only a memory.

And he was filled.

Melkhjert seemed happy too; she dropped her head and sighed.

A deep, contented feeling overtook Torbjorn, and his eyelids grew heavy. There was nothing more he wanted than to sleep. Then Smakkerdette mooed and looked at him painfully.

She needed him too. *Storfjell needs me*, he thought. So he crawled over to the spotted cow and milked her. From her udder there came the same thing: instead of milk, rich, creamy butter.

Torbjorn nearly laughed at how all of it. He milked a fresh glob of butter into his hand, then smeared it across Storfjell's lips.

The gigantic man's mouth pursed together, and he swallowed. His face relaxed, and color flowed into the loose, grey skin under his eyes again. Then his tongue licked across his lips searching for more, so that Storfjell for that moment reminded Torbjorn of Smakkerdette.

Torbjorn milked Smakkerdette again, then fed his brother more, smearing the shining butter across his lips and into his mouth. Storfjell did not wake, but he swallowed, and Torbjorn wondered if Storfjell were half dreaming, half awake.

Torbjorn continued his task until finally Storfjell smacked his lips, smiled wide, and turned on his side. He began to snore.

Smakkerdette ambled over to Melkhjert and nuzzled her, then rested her chin on Melkhjert's shoulder and went to sleep.

Torbjorn felt oh-so-tired and happy. He did not have the strength to care what may come. Even if he'd tried, he could not walk another step, and finally, he too collapsed, closed his eyes and let sleep overcome him. Meanwhile, high up on the ridge, the trolls were searching for a way down the snowy mountain.

Chapter 14 — The Buttersmiths' Gold

Torbjorn felt something from high up on the mountain calling him. He could not remember where he was, but he knew he'd been there a long time and that he'd never been so happy. In his dream his belly was full. He had the vague sense that he was lying in a feather bed as tall as a house. The Nine Churns surrounded him. His clan stood at his side, singing soft, melodic songs that he hadn't heard since he was cradled as a baby in his Mother's arms. He wasn't sure, but it felt like he'd been asleep for a thousand years.

The voice on the mountaintop came down and called again. This time it was in his face. "Torbjorn!" The voice pulled him up and out of the feather bed.

Then the voice shook him, and he felt hot breath on his face. "Torbjorn!" it shouted. Torbjorn recognized it. *Storfjell*. His brother.

"You must wake up!" Storfjell said. Suddenly, Torbjorn was at the foot of the mountain again. He forced his heavy eyelids open. There was Storfjell, his helmet fixed to his head, his eyes sharp and fierce.

"Torbjorn, it is the middle of the night!" Storfjell said. The moon was high in the sky still – higher than it had been before. How long had Torbjorn slept? "It is a wonder the trolls are not already upon us!"

With that, all the peace and rest Torbjorn felt fled, and familiar panic returned to his chest. He propped himself up on his elbows. It was dark.

A loud, guttural growl echoed through the forest from behind a copse of trees just to the north of them.

"They are here!" cried Storfjell.

Torbjorn leapt to his feet. It was easier than he expected after such a long sleep, and he turned his head this way and that, looking for the bovines.

The two of them were standing under a tree nearby, between Torbjorn and the sound of the troll. They turned round and round, stamping the ground. He could see terror in their wide eyes.

"Brother, we must run this way!" said Storfjell, pointing to an opening in the forest away from the copse of trees.

Just then, the red troll smashed through the trees behind the bovines. It roared so loud, pine needles shook and the air shivered. It was so close that for the first time, Torbjorn could see into its open jaws. Its teeth were long and blunt at the end, like the horns of a bull that had been ground across rock and stone. Gravel crumbled out of its gums. Its tongue was wide as a shovel's head and covered in warts. The needle-like hairs on its back stood on end, like an angry dog's that was ready to fight.

He could not leave Melkhjert. Without thinking, Torbjorn darted between the troll and her. He picked her up with both arms and to his surprise, she was lighter than usual, so he slung her under one arm and scooped up Smakkerdette with the other. Then, with a bovine under each arm, he charged away from the troll as fast as he could.

He could have sworn the ground was flat, but he felt like he was flying downhill again, his legs moved so easily.

He flew by Storfjell, and with one strong heave, tossed Smakkerdette into the air at his brother. "Catch," Torbjorn said, surprised at himself. He was even more surprised at how Smakkerdette flew into Storfjell's open arms.

Storfjell caught her with a grunt and chased after Torbjorn, his legs beating like dragonfly wings.

They flew across the small clearing in no time, passed the trees, and were just about to reach a pile of boulders on the other side when the rocks at the top of the pile shattered to pieces in a deafening crack. He veered left, away from the sound.

The huge, grey-colored troll leapt down from the stack of boulders onto the ground. He pounded both huge fists into the dirt and snarled at the forest all around him. The earth quaked under Torbjorn's feet. The birds in the trees cried shrill and loud and flapped away by the flock, and suddenly Torbjorn had nowhere to go.

There were only a few yards of open ground between him and the grey troll. Storfjell stood next to him, with Smakkerdette under his arm. There was nowhere to run. It was time to stand.

Torbjorn set down Melkhjert in the dirt, threw back his cloak, and drew his knife from his belt. Storfjell dropped Smakkerdette and drew his battle axe.

Torbjorn placed his hand in the short fur on Melkhjert's back. It was comforting, for that one moment, to feel her breath go in and out, as fast as it was, and to know that her heart was beating inside her. Torbjorn had never heard of a man fighting a troll. He'd only heard of the end result: the troll grinding the man's bones in its jaws. What had so often been just stories was now his fate.

The grey troll leapt forward and came crashing down in front of Torbjorn. It raised both its fists over its head, like it was about to swing them down on top of Torbjorn's skull.

Torbjorn remembered what Storfjell had said about loving one's clan. He crouched. "BATTLE!" he cried, with the full force and fury of his hardened life in the snows and icy waves of the North.

And then Torbjorn felt something hit him hard from behind. It was like a house had fallen on him from the side, so large was the blow. It knocked him in the back, shoulders, arms and legs all simultaneously, so that he flew past the grey troll through the air and smashed into the stack of boulders.

The boulders hit him even harder than the blow from behind. The forest flashed red and all the air was knocked from his lungs; he was certain, from the pain, that his ribs had been crushed flat too. *I am broken*, thought Torbjorn, knowing that a blow like that was sure to shatter his bones.

He slid off the boulder onto the ground. He lay on the earth and tried to force the spinning, blurry forest to stop. He rolled awkwardly on his front, pushed up with his arms, and to his surprise, was able to stand.

Torbjorn looked at his hands. They were scratched, but unbroken. He took a deep breath, and though he felt his lungs were only half full, there was a surge of life inside him. He was alive.

He looked back. The red troll crouched in the clearing where Torbjorn had been moments before. It had hit him from behind. Melkhjert was gone.

There was a gasp of pain. The grey troll seized Storfjell by the neck with both of its gigantic, three-fingered hands and lifted him in the air. Storfjell's battle axe lay on the ground below his feet. He clutched at the troll's wrists, struggling to breathe.

"Brother!" Torbjorn cried. He wrenched a boulder twice the size of his head free from the stack – he'd never been able to lift one that size before – with both arms Torbjorn heaved the boulder over his head at the grey troll.

The boulder flew through the air and smashed the troll at the base of its head and crumbled into pieces. The troll roared up at the sky, dropping Storfjell and writhing and clawing at the back of its head like an injured snake.

"Fiend!" Torbjorn cried. He had never expected to insult a troll to its face. But ever since he'd woken up from his sleep, his belly still glowed inside him, and there was something in his arms and legs that gave him strength, as if the golden butter had coated his innards with life. He felt nothing less than mighty.

The grey troll's eyes were squinty, and it was still beating itself on the head and thrashing at the ground in pain. The red troll crouched low, creeping its way across the earth toward Torbjorn, its eyes pouring red hot heat out their sockets. The bovines were nowhere to be seen.

Torbjorn clattered up the stack of boulders and seized a tree branch as thick as his arm that hung nearby. He slid one hand up the branch toward the trunk, and heaving all his weight downward, yanked it with both arms. The wood splintered, then broke. He wrenched the branch free. He could not have done that before – not without the strength of the golden butter in his bones.

The red troll leapt at him first. Torbjorn dodged to his right. It missed him by a hand's breadth and skidded across the boulder top.

The grey troll swiped at his leg from the other side, catching Torbjorn by the ankle and knocking him off his footing. Torbjorn steadied himself, then swung the stout branch with both arms like a club. He caught the grey troll full in the face. Its face crumpled, the blow knocking the troll backward. It squealed in pain.

Then Torbjorn felt a tug at his ankle, and he was yanked off his feet backwards and swung over the rocks to the ground behind. In the instant Torbjorn was in the air, he saw two things: the red troll beneath him, throwing him by the ankles, and a cliff a few arm lengths away with a lake below. *Strange, the moonlight on the water looks so beautiful*, he thought. He slammed against the dirt.

"Storfjell!" he coughed, forcing himself to ignore the pain. He wasn't sure where Storfjell was. The red troll charged, its teeth bared and its tongue slithering as it hissed hot, steamy breath at Torbjorn.

"We can defeat the foes!" he cried, even as he rolled, and the red troll's fists smashed the ground right next to him. There was strength inside Torbjorn now beyond any a Smordaler ever possessed. They could not give up, not now that mighty strength surged through their bones.

The red troll lashed out again, swiping at Torbjorn's head. This time Torbjorn caught its arm in his hands. Its skin was rough like broken stone on his palms. He pulled, twisting and throwing his weight downward. The troll was incredibly heavy, but Torbjorn pulled with such fury that the troll tumbled over his back and with a heave, he threw it off the edge of the cliff.

Torbjorn looked down at the lake. It wasn't far to the water below. Probably only half the length of a longboat. But it was too far for the troll. It splashed into the deep, blue water and sank out of sight. A burst of bubbles and steam rose up where the troll had broken the water's surface. From there, small waves radiated out into the lake and died away.

Torbjorn sighed. Trolls can't cross water. To drown in it was doom.

Torbjorn turned, and his moment of triumph faded. Right behind him stood the huge grey troll, blocking his escape. He did not think he had *that* much strength to throw the large one.

"Duck!" cried Storfjell. Torbjorn did not know what his brother would do – there was no time to ask. Torbjorn flattened himself on the ground.

A huge log swung horizontally at the troll, catching it squarely in the back. The troll fell forward, landing face-first in the dirt. It twisted like a snake, brought its gaping jaws backward and upward and bit down Storfjell's arm.

"Beeegawwwwwwww!" wailed Storfjell. He wrestled to break free, but the troll's grip was too strong. It shook its head back and forth like a hound, whipping Storfjell into a nearby tree like a ragged doll.

"Storfjell!" cried Torbjorn. He leapt to his feet and flung himself onto the troll's back. Storfjell's arm was still clamped in the beast's monstrous jaws.

The grey troll clawed over his shoulders at Torbjorn's back. Torbjorn held tightly, then, caring nothing for his own limbs, rammed his fingers like spear heads into the troll's mouth.

He felt hot, sticky spit smear across his hands. His fingers dug into gravelly gums until he found a pair of blunt teeth. Then, using all the strength of Smordal and the magic of the golden butter inside him, he pried the jaws of the troll slowly apart one inch. It was like splitting apart a boulder with bare hands, the troll's tongue writhing and scraping across his fingers, trying to break his hold while its claws struck at Torbjorn's back. He held on, and pulled all the harder, giving every ounce of might in his bones, until there was a crack, and the troll's jaws flapped open wide.

Storfjell wrenched his arm free. He fell to the ground. The troll screamed so shrilly, it was like the rocks inside his belly had split open and shot out into the night. It teetered, then fell onto Storfjell.

Exhausted, Torbjorn set his shoulder against the beast and shoved it toward the cliff. It rolled over, and Storfjell kicked out his legs against the troll's belly. "By Thor's hammer, push!" shouted Storfjell. Torbjorn shoved again. It was not enough. The troll was too heavy.

There was a rustle in the trees. Smakkerdette and Melkhjert came charging out of the forest. They lowered their heads, and in unison, rammed the troll.

It skidded over the cliff, clawing at the edge as it went tumbling down to the water below.

Torbjorn fell back onto the ground. Hot tears came to his eyes. Storfjell lay on the ground behind him, a great big pine tree as thick as a sheep at his head. It was still green, and its roots were covered in fresh dirt. Storfjell must have ripped it out of the ground.

"Brother, we have vanquished the foes!" Storfjell said, holding his arm limply. He was grinning so wide his mustache did not hide it this time. His teeth looked like a row of polished white rocks.

Torbjorn peered over the edge of the cliff. There was no sign of either troll, only bubbles and steam.

He let out a long whistle. "Yah! And you have also vanquished that tree!" he said.

Storfjell patted the pine he'd ripped out of the ground. "Then let that be a lesson to all the forest," he said grinning, "that none shall stand against the mighty brothers."

"Nor their bovines!" said Torbjorn. He patted Melkhjert's ear. Melkhjert licked his hand.

Storfjell's warm, orange complexion had returned to his cheeks, and he seemed to glow as if the moon were shining just on him. "Do you feel good, my brother?" asked Torbjorn.

"Yah! My bones are like iron bones, and my tummy is made of happiness. I've had the most delicious dream."

Torbjorn wanted to laugh. Storfjell had not realized what he'd eaten. "I will tell you a story, Brother, that will boggle your forehead," said Torbjorn. "But we have a long walk ahead of us in which I will say it."

Chapter 15 — Mercy

It took two and a half days before Storfjell and Torbjorn finally found their way. The snow had not come in this part of the country, which made the walking easier and let the bovines graze whenever they found crispy grass. Torbjorn told Storfjell all that had happened with the butter inside the cows. They ate it often when they stopped to rest.

They wrapped Storfjell's arm in a sling made of Torbjorn's cloak. It was probably broken. It had been shot with an arrow, and even worse, chewed on by a troll, but Storfjell did not complain. He knew how lucky he was to be alive.

They followed the moss on the rocks, which always grew on one side, until they found a river Father had taught them about that flowed from the high meadows in the woods. The going was easy this time, since whenever they tired, they could stop to milk butter from the bovines.

By the second day, the creamy butter had thinned into clear, white milk again, just as before.

"Torbjorn! Do you suppose that we joggled these bovines so much with our tumbling down the hill, their moo-ish nectar churned to buttery gold inside their udders?" asked Storfjell.

That was exactly what Torbjorn had been thinking. "Yah! It must be," he said. "But do not forget, my brother, that we also joggled them up and down on our shoulders as we ran for many miles through the forest."

Storfjell said, "And now without so much joggling, their butter is white and thin again." Storfjell scratched his beard thoughtfully and got a faraway look, like his mind was thinking about many tomorrows to come.

"Brother!" said Torbjorn. "Burning the Nine Churns was an act of wisdom. But you did not know how wise you were!"

Storfjell's distant stare broke. He smiled. "Perhaps we should find more things to burn down then, if it always turns out so nice."

Torbjorn punched his brother in the good arm. He had not dared to do so before, but this time it was Storfjell who needed scolding.

That evening, as the brothers walked in the gathering mists and the night grew grey, a tall cloaked man with a wide brimmed hat appeared in their path. Two ravens beat their wings on his shoulders. He drove his staff into the ground so forcefully, it sounded like thunder.

It was the Wanderer. "You defied me," he said.

Torbjorn put his hand on his knife. It was a useless gesture. They could not fight magic. Storfjell had defied Asgard, and now they would have to pay for their deeds.

"I have done what I've done," said Storfjell.

Then unexpectedly, the Wanderer smiled. "And a new treasure has come of your defiance, a treasure greater than a hundred churns from Asgard could make. You've forged a new destiny for Smordal, one that will last nine hundred years."

Storfjell looked at Torbjorn.

"There is great magic in loyalty – more so perhaps, than I knew before." The Wanderer glanced at the two bovines. "Go," he said. "Make peace with your father. Your clan needs this gift."

Torbjorn opened his mouth to protest. He was confused. He'd been prepared for the Wanderer's wrath, and just like that, they'd been pardoned.

"There is something far greater in store for your Golden Treasure than you know. One day, someone will come for it. Save it for those who are noble and good," he said.

And then he was gone.

They'd been forgiven. There was nothing to discuss. Torbjorn and Storfjell knew what they had seen and what had been said. They simply turned toward the direction where the sun would rise.

One day later they spotted a new village in the distance between two hills. A high wall of sharpened logs rose up out of the ground, their points aimed at the sky. The wall was so wide it looked like it surrounded more than one longhouse, and judging from the trails of smoke that wafted skyward, the village must have been twice the size of the village in Smordal. A green banner hung from the walls.

There were cattle and men and women outside the walls, and lean-tos and cooking fires scattered down the hill, like someone was camping there. Even from a distance he recognized it: it was the herd of Smordal. The clan must have found its way to this village; the villagers must have offered them refuge.

Inside Torbjorn's heart was happy – then his throat tightened, and he feared. This was the clan that had exiled them as traitors.

Storfjell must have seen his fear. He placed a steady hand on Torbjorn's shoulder. "We have news for them," he said.

A large man outside the walls turned and ran toward them. He raised his hand and hailed them.

"Father," Torbjorn said.

"My sons," Father said. He smiled so wide, his hay-colored beard parted down the middle. Soon, they would taste butter as a clan once again.

Chapter 16 — Golden Destiny

"And that is how we gave up butter churns centuries ago. Everything changed for our people then," said today's Torbjorn to Braxton as he finished his story on board their ship. He stood up from the barrel he sat on and patted the young cow that pulled at the oars. The telling of such a tale seemed to have tired him.

"Well now ain't that a hummmmdinger," said the old pilot Braxton. "Then how did you end up with the same exact names as those two ancient fellas?"

"Easy!" said Storfjell. "Our father gave them to us! Ever since they learned to joggle the bovines the clan has named *somebody* in each generation after the greatest Smordaler that ever lived! There has been a Storfjell and Torbjorn ever since."

"After that, there were many who came looking for the Golden Fortune of our herds," said Torbjorn. "They sailed up and down the coast, raiding and plundering villages. To stay hidden, our clan moved away to an island out in the sea where no one could find them."

"Bjørnøya," said Braxton. It was the same island where he'd met Torbjorn and Storfjell in the first place.

"After learning to joggle the bovines our people began to live very long lives. Longer than a hundred years. Something had changed in the butter, and that something changed *us*," said Torbjorn. "Some even lived to be twice as old as a tree."

It was remarkable, Braxton had to admit, that these boys were already in their eighties. They looked so young. "But wasn't that Wanderer angry with those fellas? He had something grand planned for that butter after all," asked Braxton.

Torbjorn turned. "But joggled butter is so delicious!" he said, scooping a glob of golden butter from the barrel.

"There was another messenger that came to our fathers, before we were born," said Storfjell. "He was not the Wanderer as we knew him, or perhaps he was the Wanderer in a different form. The Master Mead-Maker, they called him. He told them the same thing, that with the Golden Fortune of our Herds, violent men would beat their swords into cooking pots and the roar of the dragons would cease."

Storfjell said then, quietly, "I believe now that the promise still holds."

"He told our fathers of a city far away that he was to build where that promise would come true. In it the Master Mead Maker would gather the tastes of the world," said Torbjorn. "It was to be a city of delicious taste."

"That is why your Warmlander friends must not fail," said Storfjell.

"The Johnsonvilles," whispered Braxton to himself. It pained him to think how far away they must be. He did not know what had happened to them.

"I believe this Guster, the one with the all-searching tongue, he is brave," said Torbjorn.

"Not to mention how feisty that mother of his can get," Braxton said.

He pulled back his cap, ran his fingers through his wispy grey hair and let out a long whistle. There was a lot there to chew on. "You know, I'd never heard a tale so tall that it couldn't reach knee-high to a grasshopper until today," he said. "I don't know which one is harder to believe – trolls and cows or this city of taste."

"How about men sitting inside great silver birds and this funny weaving you wear?" said Torbjorn, pointing at Braxton's clothes.

Braxton laughed. Torbjorn was talking about his plane. The plane certainly must have seemed as strange to the two giant Buttersmiths as their story seemed to Braxton.

"We will take you to the Warmlands," said Torbjorn. "And there you must find the Johnsonvilles."

"I will," said Braxton. He had to help them if he could.

And with that, he ate another blueberry muffin. Storfjell and Torbjorn ate seventeen more apiece.

Find out what happens to Guster and the Johnsonvilles in
Book 2 of the Evertaster Series. Coming soon:

The Delicious City

ABOUT THE AUTHOR

In between books, Adam Glendon Sidwell uses the power of computers to make monsters, robots and zombies come to life for blockbuster movies such as *Pirates of the Caribbean*, *King Kong*, *I, Robot* and *Tron*. Long ago he spent two years wandering the land of the Vikings without being slain, so feels very qualified to write this book. He once met a Norwegian with 1,000 neckties. For the time being, Adam lives in Los Angeles with his wife and daughter, where he can't wait for the big one to hit.

Say hello to Adam here: www.evertaster.com

Want Adam to come to your school? Contact:
publicity@evertaster.com

Join the Antics!

www.facebook.com/evertaster   www.youtube.com/evertaster

Bring Adam to your school!
Email publicity@evertaster.com